DEATH
on the
MOON

By

Jeanne Maree Iacono

DEATH
on the
MOON

By

Jeanne Maree Iacono

Lunada Press, LLC

www.deathonthemoon.com

This is a work of fiction. Names, characters, businesses, places, events, locales, and incidents are either the products of the author's imagination or used in a fictitious manner. Any resemblance to actual persons, living or dead, or actual events is purely coincidental and not intended by the author.

NASA is used freely as a government agency throughout the work, however, this story is fictitious and does not imply these missions have occurred in the past or will be functional in the future.

~ Jeanne Maree Iacono

Lunada Press, LLC

ISBN 13: 978-0937176-11-5

In memory of my brother, Bob,
who loved to fly at night
and look down at Earth
through the star and moon light.

ACKNOWLEDGEMENTS

Thank you to Keith for the initial support and encouragement to combine my love of writing mystery with an adventure to the moon.

Thank you to Glenn who discussed the future of mankind and space exploration with me while offering continued support.

Thank you to Donna Burke for her assistance in the process of editing, and to Tim Hurley for creating great artwork for the front and back covers.

Thank you to my friends Bernadette, Carolyn, Don, John, Marlene, Mary and Nancy who always enthusiastically encourage me to follow my dream and write.

A very special thank you to Jeannie Rose, my granddaughter, for her advice about "time" which inspired me to complete this novel.

*"We set sail on this new sea because there is new
knowledge to be gained, and new rights to be won,
and they must be won and used for the progress of
all people. For space science, like nuclear science
and all technology, has no conscience of its own.
Whether it will become a force for good or ill
depends on man... "*

"We Choose To Go To The Moon!"

~ John F. Kennedy
September 12, 1962
Rice University Stadium

PROLOGUE

Our actions, good or evil, transcend our Earth now and multiply on our moon before returning to us as our results, Robin Mulvaina typed in bold across the bottom edge of the calendar that was embedded inside the body of a turquoise square at the lower right-hand corner of his sleek computerized desktop. He felt pensive, even philosophical. He looked up and realized the room had darkened while he had been deep in his thoughts. The day was done. It was time to leave the office. Mulvaina moved his forefinger forward to the turquoise calendar and tapped his finger twice on the day's date highlighting it. The date expanded into a larger neat turquoise square box. Mulvaina typed three words. Johnson Electrical Company.

"Now go to sleep," he said with a command and the large square shrunk down to nothing and his desktop faded to a solid dark grey. As Mulvaina stood up to leave his office, he knew from an old instinctive feeling that the night was just beginning.

CHAPTER 1

SANTA FE SPRINGS
County of Los Angeles
2030 A.D.

For Los Angeles and its surrounding communities, nighttime was like a fortune-teller. It reminded its inhabitants of the haunting past and showed them a glimpse of the ever-evolving future. This was especially true in the older downtown industrial areas and tonight was no exception. Empty asphalt parking lots and old concrete warehouses created an eerie maze. In nearby storage lots, robotic security dogs lifted their heads to the starless sky and howled a long forgotten sound.

Somewhere from out of the darkness, a late model black van, headlights extinguished, maneuvered slowly forward until it stopped in front of a large metal warehouse garage door marked in tall letters JOHNSON ELECTRICAL COMPANY. Three men wearing dark overalls, their heads covered in dark caps, jumped out of the van and rushed towards the door. A short bear-like man pressed his booted foot against the door, inserted a key into the lock, then with slow careful guidance, rolled the door up with minimal sound. The men stepped inside. Inside was darker than night. The bear-like man squinted trying to adjust his eyes, then after a few brief seconds, he motioned the van inside. He surveyed the parking lots and cross-streets as far as his eyes could reach. No one. Nothing. Satisfied, he brought the warehouse door down slowly and quietly.

Four flashlights ruptured the darkness. Light panned from wall to wall. Metal boxes stood stacked five feet high on wide steel pallets. The bear-like man searched labels up and down the pallets until, "Here," his hush voice commanded, "Take this one. And Snout, these three."

The men worked at loading the van with determined speed. No one spoke but in the brief moments that stretched like hours, there came a muffled sound. A sound, not like feet moving against floor. Not like the sliding of a box. But a sound that caused Snout to strain to see through the darkness. He raised his eyes towards the rafters. He felt danger around him like a shroud. He set his metal box down carefully. His flashlight began to pan the rafters. Suddenly the light illuminated a hulking shadow. It moved upright. The sense of danger climaxed in a minute's second. Snout quickly reached to draw his weapon from the holster strapped around his underarm, but it was too late. A dart ripped into his chest. He dropped to the floor silently screaming with pain, but mostly from utter terror of being sparked to death. His body contorted with convulsions.

The other men stared in dumb fear but only for a second. They turned off their flashlights, dropped their boxes, and ran for the van. In the darkness the van engine started up in a frenzied pitch. "Let's get the hell out of here," hollered the bear-like man.

The driver instantaneously shifted into reverse and gunned the accelerator. The van's bumper bulldozed through the metal door then burst into pieces as the van collided into a barrier of squad cars that had been positioned into place just moments earlier.

Interior warehouse lights went on with full intensity. From behind the boxes a dozen policemen, FBI, Homeland Security agents, and a few civilian observers emerged. Quickly the officers pulled the dazed occupants out of the van, handcuffed them, and pushed them to the center of the warehouse where Snout still lay, his arms wrapped tight around his chest, uttering, "No more sparks. No more sparks."

George Carver, standing straight and strong in his six foot-two, black forty frame, dominated the warehouse as he shouted the order to the other law enforcement agents, "Right now, one of you guys, turn the sparkler off and get that man up and over here with the rest of these men."

A man approximately in his late thirties, dressed in casual

grey slacks and a solid maroon V-neck sweater approached him. "Lucky night, wouldn't you say? This will get you noticed," he said addressing Carver.

Carver smiled just a little, then in a dominating tone said, "I don't rely on that old superstition of Lady Luck. Nothing more than a false conception of causation. It's careful planning, Mulvaina. You ready now to talk to these scumbags?"

Mulvaina nodded affirmatively. Together they walked over to the apprehended men. For a few seconds they just stood silently staring at the men. Mulvaina at last said rather tauntingly, "It sure is strange how you seem to keep showing up at interesting and peculiar places, Salvo."

Salvo's eyes burned. "So, this Mulvaina is how you make your living by kissing up to agents. You may think you are a smart private dick but someday I'll get you." Salvo made a coarse throaty sound and spat a mouthful of saliva at Mulvaina and Carver.

Both men jumped backwards. "Did any get on you?" hollered a police officer.

Two other officers quickly slipped on rubber gloves. "Disgusting asshole," one of them said under his breath. They grabbed Salvo and began to lead him out of the warehouse.

"Listen to me Mulvaina, someday you'll pay," Salvo hollered as he twisted his head back throwing a threatening face to Mulvaina. Then Salvo suddenly changed his tone and said in a calm matter-of-fact way, "Officers, it's not necessary to wrinkle my clothes. I'm coming along in a cooperative manner. I want to look good when my lawyer arrives and gets your badges." Salvo raised his voice and emphasized his words, "For false arrest. I was hired to make a pick-up here. You'll see."

"Wait," ordered Carver. "Are you saying, Salvo, that you have permission from Johnson Electrical Company to enter their warehouse tonight?"

"I've got the key in my pocket," answered Salvo.

"Which pocket?" asked Carver.

"Front left," said Salvo with a dead pan voice.

Carver motioned for one of the young police officers to get the key. The warehouse seemed to hold its breath in anticipation. The officer reached his arm down into the overall pant pocket and tunneled down against the side of Salvo's leg, and then in one yank upward he retrieved the key. The officer quickly brought it over to Carver and then took a guarding stance next to Salvo.

Holding it between his forefingers, Carver dangled the key in the air. "Is this the key you're talking about?" he asked.

"Yea, that looks like it," answered Salvo.

"Who authorized tonight's pick-up and who gave you this key?" asked Carver firing the question in a loud, thunderous tone.

"Don Pixley," said Salvo as he turned an angry glare at Mulvaina.

Carver looked at Mulvaina and simply nodded affirmation. Then, without a word, Mulvaina walked over to the van and talked for a few seconds with the men checking the contents of the wrecked vehicle. Soon Mulvaina and a tall man with a sandy blond moustache and rimless glasses came forward and joined Carver. The three men conferred for a moment, then the tall man asked Salvo, "Do you know what is contained inside these metal storage boxes you're picking up?"

"I'm just getting what I'm authorized to pick up," answered Salvo smugly.

"And who authorized you to pick up this particular load of Helium III Detectors?" the tall man fired back.

"Don Pixley," answered Salvo.

The tall man took off his glasses, and stared without emotion at Salvo. "I am Don Pixley, and I don't know who in the hell you are."

Salvo stood stunned. His face grayed.

"I certainly did not authorize you to pick up anything from this warehouse," Pixley continued with authority.

Quickly recovering Salvo said, "There's something fucked up here. I need to talk to my lawyer right now."

Carver gave the command, "Read him his rights and take him and these other men down to the station."

The young officer began reciting the rights passage in a monotone voice as if being forced to recite a well-known prayer he no longer believed in. He pushed Salvo into the nearest squad car. As soon as he slammed the door shut, the squad car instantly sped away into the dark night.

"Thank you, Mr. Pixley for your help," said Mulvaina. "I think we have an air-tight case. We have as you might say, caught them in the act."

"We certainly did, and I know Mr. Johnson will be pleased when he hears about your efficient action. You know, it was obvious that Salvo didn't know the significance of what he was picking up," said Pixley.

The two men exchanged handshakes then, Don Pixley walked over to where the main light switch was located and flipped it off. The warehouse succumbed to a shadowy existence once again.

Mulvaina and Carver walked to where a few more squad cars waited. A young policeman ran over and opened the back door of one of the cars and held it open for Carver. "Get some rest. And thanks for cooperating with us on breaking up this black market thievery," said Carver.

"We should be able to make this one stick on Salvo," said Mulvaina.

"Salvo. Shit. Who knows with his lawyer? He's a real bulldog against our Homeland Security legislation. But, you can bet on one thing," said Carver with disgust, "that bastard will be out on bail before the damn sun is up."

"You think so?"

"Hey. You're not worried about his threat?" asked Carver.

"Hell no," retorted Mulvaina. "I've got more important crap to worry about. I'm going back to the office right now and get my report for Johnson Electric Company finished along with their final billing."

"Yea, you private investigators are always keeping track of those greenbacks," Carver said with a slight smile. Carver gestured farewell with his two forefingers solely for Mulvaina's benefit as the squad car sped away.

Mulvaina knew he had to head back to his office to write up his report of the night's events while the specifics could still be recalled clearly and accurately and without losing even a slight detail that perhaps could, at a later time, turn out to have significance in the case.

He walked across the deserted street to another parking lot where he had camouflaged his car between two old large dump trucks. "Another long night at the detective desk," he said under his breath.

"Another long night alone," his mind's voice interjected.

He pushed back the voice and decided he needed to grab a cheeseburger and a black coffee. Using voice command Mulvaina told his car to head straight for the nearest burger drive-thru.

As Mulvaina pulled his burger and coffee through the window he surmised that the fast food drive-thru was man's true time link to the past and future.

CHAPTER 2

Mulvaina and Helms opened the car rear doors and got inside. Mulvaina reached forward towards the car's side paneled door and touched the computer screen and typed in Barish International. "Departure in three minutes. Please fasten all safety devices," a voice commanded. Both men buckled up. Helms pushed a button on the side of his seat and put himself in a reclining position.

"Rough night," Mulvaina aksed?

"I'd say," Helms replied. "The wife had the flu and I cooked dinner, washed up dishes, and read bed-time stories about pigs and bears, wild little creatures and fairy godmothers into the late hours of the night. I tell you it's hard being a family man. Be glad your single, man."

With all of the complaining Mulvaina could hear the love in Helm's family man voice and he felt a tinge of jealousy. Mulvaina sat straight but turned towards the screen. He tapped a red button and turned up the volume. Then he pressed the button labeled "visual" and began to enjoy the beautiful face of Rita Noble along with the sound of her mesmerizing voice. He looked at the bottom of the screen to catch the morning news. Locally, the fundraiser for the new L.A. community children's playground labyrinth project had raised $75,000 through a number of event activities. Next scrolling along the screen was a historic note: Dating back over 3,500 years, labyrinths have been linked with health benefits. Then in bullet points the screen listed benefits: A walk through a labyrinth releases worries. Labyrinth walking promotes cures. Labyrinth walking calms and lowers blood pressure. The screen changed its colored background. Next, there was a scroll announcing that surplus government commodities would be distributed to eligible families beginning the following week. Times and locations for the distribution ran across the screen. Suddenly Rita's beautiful face faded into the background and the dignified face of a man about sixty appeared. At the bottom of the screen the name Dr. John Eggleston was highlighted followed by the information: Former doctor of a major global health biotechnological company has been convicted of making false statements about the company's newest drug's effectiveness in fighting liver disease.

"I've always been suspicious of global health," said Helms as he sat up from his inclined seat position and began looking at the computer screen. "Goals of global health contain political assumptions about how the world should be organized as one single place."

"I don't know," said Mulvaina. "Everyone can have empathy with others on disease and illness regardless of their nationality and belief systems. Health issues are a commonality of being human. If we can build and live on the moon, we certainly can afford global health care. Some doctors like Eggleston are just damn corrupted by the bucks. That doesn't make the goal evil." Mulvaina paused as he looked at Helms realizing he was looking at only a mid-twenties adult, barely out in the workforce after graduating as an accountant. Here sitting next to him was a young man still in his prime athletic years who had all that male agility, strength and stamina. Mulvaina had to admit to himself that Helms had not yet reached that maturity level that reflects on personal health issues let alone made global health a personal issue.

Suddenly the woman's voice faded. The song was over. Mulvaina turned the volume down again. "Rumor has it that Rita Noble is going to win the Golden Music Award for 2035. What do you think, Helms?" Mulvaina asked.

"She has my vote," answered Helms. He cleared his throat and added, "Even if she is a damn robotic and not a real dame."

Before he could respond to Helm's comment, Mulvaina heard the familiar single clear ring tone. "It is exactly ten a.m.," said a female robotic voice. For a second Mulvaina's mind drifted back to the dining room of his mother's house. He could remember the chiming of the old oak clock that sat on top the fireplace mantle. How his mother loved that clock and repeated often how her great-great-great grandfather had brought it from Germany to America and it had passed from generations to her. She loved the sound of its chiming as the hands stood on the hours. He remembered how she cried for days when the internet sent a bulletin out to everyone's home message center declaring that all clocks not digitized were banned from households and must be brought to the recycling plant. He more clearly remembered the announcement that the possession of any non-digitized clock was a crime punishable with a fine. At the time he was too young to understand why his mother cried for days before she brought the old clock to the recycling plant. He had believed she was just too old and that it was yet another sign that she did not have the vitality to be part of the marvelous future of mankind. He remembered telling his third grade teacher about his mother's tears as she handed the clock to the robotic at the entrance of the recycling plant. Today he remembered his third grade teacher's words still with their strong clarity, "It is important for everyone to march to the same time in order to accelerate forward into the marvels and opportunities of the future."

Mulvaina had rushed inside of the house when he got home from school to tell his mother what his wise teacher had said, and today he also remembered his mother's strong words, "What good are all of the marvels of the future if we don't have freedom to keep family heirlooms to remember people we loved in the past."

Mulvaina could not understand what holding on to an old out-dated technology had to do with freedom then when his mother spoke those words. Even now he would not trade his lifestyle for anything different, but he had aged enough to think about how his mother must have felt the day she handed over her family-treasured clock to the recycling plant.

"It's ten, already," Helms interrupted his thoughts.

"We should be getting off at the next exit. That should be Flower," said Mulvaina.

A few seconds later the car smoothly slowed, turned left, then automatically picked up speed as it headed down the new street.

"I must admit," said Mulvaina, "your new autonomous car is a smooth ride. I had been thinking of getting one of the new ecojet types. Sort of appeals to me to coast at 150-plus mph."

"Yes, that's impressive," interjected Helms.

"Yes, impressive," said Mulvaina pensively. "However, some details are again not worked out even on this year's model. It still sounds like a taxiing jet at idle. I took a demonstration drive. I think it sounds loud when it is cruising just above the street surface, too, but I sure have been tempted to buy one so I can just flip a switch on the front panel and take off and fly from city to city. Think of how fast I could travel around for investigating my cases. Problem is, though, the cost is still just for the very rich."

"This is reasonably priced and it has a government approval stamp, too," said Helms with pride. "I think it's quite stylish. I like the silver chrome structure, green dominating bumpers, and the expansive side windows for viewing. I like the roof's solar panels in contrasting navy. Did you notice that the solar panels are small squares so that it adds some textured depth to the roof's top? Of course, it only comes in this color, and I suppose in a year or two, almost everyone will have one, and I won't look so striking on the road. A really great feature is the ergonomical design of the seats. I find them comfortable. By the way, did you notice that the road seems wide open this morning."

"Yes," interjected Mulvaina. "You must admit it has helped that the government just finished revamping the old sewer infrastructure to transport mail and packages via robotic messenger tubes so there aren't all the old mail and delivery trucks out clogging the streets anymore. It is in comparison wide open. You are such a romantic Helms." A little laugh escaped Mulvaina's lips.

"And you aren't a romantic dreaming of driving an ecojet," said Helms.

Both men laughed. Their laugh was broken by the robotic voice announcing, "Barish International. One mile ahead."

"Did Grogan say why Mr. Barish wanted to see us?" asked Helms.

"No," answered Mulvaina.

"Any inkling?" asked Helms.

"About Barish?"

Helms nodded affirmatively.

"I've got a hunch," said Mulvaina. "Probably has something to do with the Lunar Base Camp Project."

"Up at the Lunar B.C.? Don't you think it's about their new Stockton nuclear fusion reactor? Last time I spoke to Grogan, he wanted me to give him a recap on the last six months of operating costs on the Stockton reactor," said Helms.

"No," answered Mulvaina. Grogan indicated it was something sensitive. I feel it's about the moon base."

The car slowed as it approached a large multi-story office building then parked at the front curbside. The car's back doors automatically opened and Mulvaina and Helms stepped out. Both men tilted their heads back slightly and gazed at the top of the building. On the building's roof top, standing tall, was a large logo consisting of a world globe embossed with a bronze capital B.

"Barish International," announced Helms as if he was Mulvania's chauffeur instead of his right-hand man. Then he added, "Someday when Barish's son takes over the business, he'll probably change that logo to represent Barish Interplanetary."

"Probably," said Mulvaina.

It took less than two minutes walking from the curb to arrive at the exterior of the Barish International building. Mulvania and Helms stood in front of the building's tall glass beveled door entrance and looked straight ahead.

"Barish's Facial Recognition System welcomes you," said a feminine robotic voice and the tall glass doors opened. Mulvaina and Helms quickly stepped inside as a robotic voice began numerically to count off twenty seconds. When the voice reached fifteen, the doors began to slowly close and were once again totally sealed by the count of twenty. The voice stated, "Silent alarm activated."

Mulvaina and Helms stepped forward into the lobby. It had a modern, but grandiose architectural appearance. The floor was laid with black and white imported Italian tiles and the walls were bare white except for several stark silver elevator doors. To the right was a large Spanish stone fountain spewing water down the sides of three tiers, its base afloat with lily pads. Resting near the wall behind the fountain were several small black leather Spanish benches, their sides flanked by graceful palms planted in massive white ceramic pots. To the lobby's far left corner was a security desk manned by two officers who were monitoring video display units at a computer terminal complex. Before Mulvaina and Helms could precede another step, a robotic female voice spoke. "Good morning and welcome to Barish International. Before continuing, it is necessary that you register at our security desk where you will be given security badges and routed to your destination. Thank you for your cooperation."

"I like the voice of that robotic," muttered Helms under his breath.

"I still prefer a voice with moving red lips," whispered Mulvania just as they approached the security desk.

"Can I help you gentlemen?" said a security guard looking up from her computer monitor.

Mulvaina noticed the second guard did not lift his eyes from the video units, not even for a second of curiosity. He made a mental note; one of the newest man-like robotic models.

"My name is Robin Mulvaina. This is my associate Thomas Helms. We're here for a ten o'clock meeting with Mr. Barish."

The security guard looked at her digital watch. "Fifteen after ten o'clock," she said in a tone Mulvaina thought was reminiscent of an elementary teacher admonishing a tardy student.

Mulvaina started to offer a believable Angelino excuse but before he could even begin, the security guard in a monotone voice repeated, "Fifteen after ten o'clock, sir." Then without changing expression she added, "May I have your I.D. cards."

Mulvaina and Helms each handed the guard their plastic coated identification cards. The security guard placed them in one of the large computers labeled magnetic card reader. Soon from out of a printer machine came two plastic cards marked with the Barish International logo and the words "Visitor Pass".

"Thank you gentlemen," said the security guard in her same monotone voice as she handed the passes to Mulvaina and Helms. "Please wear these badges at all times while in our building and be sure to return them before you leave. You may now proceed to the elevator where you will receive instructions from Voice Control."

As they walked towards the elevator Mulvaina thought about how in less than five years scientists had perfected the outward features of the robotics and made them almost indistinguishable from the image of man. Their monotone voices were the still one strong characteristic that helped separate them from the human. Most likely, he surmised, this was intentional by the government scientists in order to eliminate efforts at espionage by fanatic terrorists. It also ran through his mind how in less than five years robotics had become indispensible to businesses. The government had given a two year credit incentive to buy the new robotic models and businesses loved not only the incentive, but reliable help that did not need health care, vacation time, sick and maternity leave, and motivational bonuses.

Helms pressed the elevator button. "Mr. Mulvaina and Mr. Helms," said a robotic female voice, "will you please step back and proceed to Elevator Three. Thank you."

A few seconds later Elevator Three opened to the twenty-second floor corridor. The two men exited. Mulvaina started briskly down the long windowless corridor. Helms hesitated. "Hey… hold on a second, Robin, I've got to…"

"Mr. Helms and Mr. Mulvaina," interrupted the robotic voice, "Please proceed immediately down the corridor and go to the last door on your left."

In a muffled whisper Helms said, "Robin, I need to stop and take a leak. I'll catch up." Helms turned and took a few steps towards a door marked Men's Room.

The robotic voice commanded, "Time restraints do not allow for any delays. Proceed forward to your appointment at once."

Helms sighed exasperated and somewhat embarrassed and hastened his steps to catch up with Mulvaina. "She makes Big Brother look like an advocate for individual rights," he whispered with some indignation.

Mulvaina quickly reflected on Helm's reference and slight negativity towards the robotic instruction, and then he whispered back, "The Astro-Four Security System is the most advanced in the world. Barish has it installed in all the nuclear power plants as well as at the Luna Base Camp. The system detects and tracks intruders as well as monitoring every step of employees and visitors. Let's face it, with a multi-millionaire like Barish, common threats can include not only thieves and kidnappers, but terrorist sabotaging his homes, offices, private jets, and moon facilities. Everything has to be fortified. In case there is a failure of the Astro-Four System for any reason, he probably has backup protection with his office having bullet resistant doors. And I bet he has burglar blasters so if someone does get past all the security measures in place, the blasters can release a fog or even noxious gas that can cause major confusion to intruders giving him time to escape to his heliport on the building's rooftop. Or even escape through secret passageways to a reinforced geo-thermal powered room."

"Why not," commented Helms, "multi-millionaires all have home amphitheaters and private spas. A geo-thermal bunker is just what every wealthy man should have."

As they approached a door on the corridor's left it slowly and smoothly opened. They stepped inside. "Good morning Mr. Mulvaina and Mr. Helms," said a sweet sounding voice with an undulating pitch.

"Amazing, a beautiful face with a beautiful voice," said Helms.

Mulvaina felt slightly uncomfortable with Helms'

flirtatious style. He also felt slightly jealous at the ease with which Helms struck up conversations with women. Mulvaina had difficulty forming the words fast enough in his head let alone speaking them when he came in close proximity with a pretty woman.

The room filled with soft sweet laughter. "The first encounter with the Astro-Four System can be unnerving, especially if you want to run to the rest room. I would offer you both a cup of coffee, but it's," she glanced at a large glass rimmed digital clock on the wall, "twenty-two minutes after ten and Mr. Barish and Mr. Grogan have been waiting for you." She pushed a button located underneath her large desk, and with a buzzing sound, the door to Mr. John Barish's office opened.

"Like entering a bank's safety deposit vault," muttered Helms under his breath.

A stern looking man, in his mid-seventies, with hard brown eyes and graying hair along the temples of his otherwise fully covered head of dark brown hair, was seated behind a mammoth smoky black desk embedded with an amber keyboard and symbols. Seated in a chair to his right was a slender fiftyish framed man with a face that seemed younger.

As Mulvaina and Helms entered the room, the younger man jumped to his feet. "Robin. Thomas. Good to see you once again." He turned towards the man seated. "Mr. Barish, let me introduce you to Robin Mulvaina and Thomas Helms."

Mr. Barish rose from his chair. He offered his hand to both men sizing them up as he did so. "Gentlemen." He gestured towards two chairs. "May I have Gloria bring you some coffee?"

"No, thank you," said Mulvaina.

Mr. Barish looked at Helms scrutinizing him in more depth as if trying to sum up his worth as he repeated his offer for coffee.

"I'm fine, thank you," Helms replied trying to keep his position from falling subservient to Mulvaina. After all, he thought, an accountant was just as important as a detective for Mr. Barish. Maybe even more so, since dollars and cents was what a man like Barish lived for. Yes, indeed, Mr. Barish was, in the category of men, definitely still a man whose main purpose in life was eagerness to acquire land, fortune, and now the wealth of the moon. Helms glanced at the photo-realistic architectural rendering on the wall to the left of Mr. Barish. It was a large display of the exterior Lunar Base Camp facility and it's outpost mining areas. In bold black letters at the bottom of the rendering was the title: Lunar B.C. and beneath those letters in smaller gold print was Lunar Barish Camp. Yes, Helms surmised, one moment in Barish's surroundings made it clear that this man was obsessed with money; its power, glory and kingdom. This was not a man to sit around and theorize about the geological formations of the moon, but rather a man from the older generation still amassing the opportunity for wealth that the moon afforded. Helms felt his self-esteem weaken.

Mr. Barish went back to his seat. "Mr. Grogan," he said, "shall we begin this meeting?"

"Certainly," Grogan said with a business-like intonation of respect. "Robin, I have been discussing with Mr. Barish some of your previous work for Barish International. Your record with us is excellent. You get results and get them quickly. When I showed Mr. Barish your track record, he was impressed and wanted to personally discuss with you further involvement with Barish International."

"Barish International is one of my company's most valued clients," said Mulvaina with all honesty, but also feeling pressured to return a compliment with a compliment.

"Good," said Gorgan. "I hope we can count on you to give your whole attention then to our immediate needs. In a few weeks the contract that Barish International has with NASA for the Lunar Base Camp Project is coming up for renewal. As you may know, Barish has been the prime contractor for the first private lunar project for nearly ten years, well actually since the original conception of the base. Mr. Barish always had an interest in space exploration and when the Obama Administration in 2010 opened it up to private enterprise pursuits, Mr. Barish was the first to turn his company's resources to the moon."

"Excuse me for interrupting" said Mulvaina, "but I would like to address Mr. Barish. Sir, my company's primary function is investigative. What would we have to do with contract negotiations?"

"Of course, Mr. Mulvaina, we have not asked you here to discuss contract negotiations. The matter at hand is far more...more," Mr. Barish paused it seemed to Mulvaina to select, just the right word, "more delicate. Please continue explaining," Mr. Barish said with a forward nod towards Grogan.

"What we have called you here for," continued Ted Grogan, "is to ask you to make an immediate, thorough, and confidential investigation of the management at Lunar B.C., and let me emphasize the word immediate. We have had some problems on the moon and we need to get to the bottom of the entire matter before NASA begins asking some embarrassing questions publicly. Time is of the essence especially now with contract renewal decisions being made soon."

"Are you trying," asked Helms, "to tell us that your lunar project is beginning to operate in the red?"

"No," said Mr. Barish quickly. "Our involvement on the moon is not forcing bankruptcy on Barish International. We never took on the lunar project with an eye for immediate high profit."

Helms responded mentally to the selective words high and immediate. Yes, Helms thought, Mr. Barish is one of a few who survived the last great depression in the first part of the twenty-first century, and now is part of the real money ruling class driving the future.

"We took," continued Mr. Barish, "the moon project on for a combination of engineering challenge and prestige. Top priority of the Lunar B.C. Project is the building of a complete colony establishment that can be used as a base for further explorations of the moon, mining resources from the moon, facilitating capture of solar energy, and of course, providing a stepping stone to Mars."

Well, Mulvania thought, Barish had well-defined and all encompassing goals for a moon base.

"Moreover," continued Mr. Barish, "the continued issuance

of contracts by government and the multitude of small, competing enterprises springing up to service the colony, like the new rocket shipping companies, assures that space is definitely the major frontier for capital investment." Mr. Barish paused letting the tips of his fingers meet and form a mock pyramid upon his desk, and then stated with a genuine historic reflection, "Remember gentlemen, since its greatness began in 1776 with the American Revolution, America has been a country of unlimited potential. It was developed by individuals with initiative and determination. Washington, Jefferson, Lincoln, Franklin, Ford, Edison, Bell, Einstein, Steve Jobs, Patton, Eisenhower, Susan B. Anthony, Wright Brothers, Amelia Earhart, Salk. The list is endless. America has led the world into the future and it will be the same for the development of the moon and other planets. America will be there first and then take mankind up as its tourists, global partners, and fellow planetary citizens. It is in our history and it is our unique mission now today, for we are surly living in the future."

He'll be making a campaign speech for president next, thought Helms.

Mr. Barish looked in Grogan's direction.

"To continue," said Grogan, "the Lunar B.C. Project means unlimited opportunities for Barish International in the century ahead. Unlimited opportunities," Grogan stressed, "unless we get a black eye on this project. In that case the effect would be disastrous on the future of the company. Do you understand?"

"Certainly," answered Mulvaina. "What kind of problem are you having?"

"We are not exactly certain," said Mr. Barish.

Grogan picked up two sets of papers off the top of Mr. Barish's desk and handed one set to Mulvaina and the other to Helms. "Here is a brief rundown of the major problem areas. In short, you'll see that the problems, and I emphasize the plural of the word, fall into three categories: inconsistent handling of funds, abnormally high expenditures and deficiencies, and last but not least, quality control. You'll also see in the report that we've had a few construction failures which we succeeded in keeping from the press. Just last month, a main girder for a pre-stress roof framework system exploded before even half of the required force had been applied."

"I see," said Mulvaina. "Multiple problems. If you suspect embezzlement, Thomas will pinpoint it. The overall investigation I will do personally. So where do we begin?"

"With our Assistant Project Manager, Carl Soots," said Grogan. "He's landing on tonight's shuttle. He's bringing documents he told us he hopes will be helpful in the investigation."

Mr. Barish abruptly stood up. "Mr. Mulvaina I look forward to working with you. I want you to begin immediately by meeting Mr. Soots right at the space port. I don't want a second lost once he steps back onto Earth. Are my intentions understood?"

"Yes, Mr. Barish the time factor will be no problem. We will be there," said Mulvaina.

"Very good," said Mr. Barish. "And let me impress upon you, Mr. Mulvaina, the management at Lunar B.C. is comprised of some of our most senior and most respected employees. My own son-in-law is in charge of lunarcrete production. I don't want any fingers wagged or accusations made without my explicit knowledge and complete authorization. Do I make myself clear, do you understand me?" said Mr. Barish with authority.

"Completely, Sir," answered Mulvaina feeling somewhat disturbed by Mr. Barish's attitude.

With finality, Mr. Barish nodded affirmatively as he once again scrutinized Mulvaina, and then without another word he walked out of the room.

"Robin, can we work under our existing monetary agreements?" asked Ted Grogan.

"Our current fees are acceptable for the investigative work. We'll need all expenses for travel back and forth from the moon reimbursed. Also, I would like a letter of authorization for all investigative work for this assignment from you for our files," said Robin.

"Certainly. I'll have Gloria type it up right now. We'll e-mail it over to your office later if you don't want to wait for it."

"That's fine Ted," said Mulvaina. He turned towards Helms. "Are we ready to go?"

"Sorry your meeting with Mr. Barish was so brief," Grogan interjected almost apologetically.

"It's totally understandable. We were late," said Mulvaina.

"I'm glad you are going to be involved in this investigation Robin," said Grogan. "I really pushed to get you on this case. I've detected a great amount of hesitancy on Mr. Barish's part to meet these lunar base problems head on. Maybe he's just getting old and tired, losing his vitality, but if it wasn't for my urging that these matters need totally cleaning up to maintain NASA's confidence, I think the man would just let things slide and be buried."

"Christ, the man's in his late seventies. He's worked hard. Built an empire in the old days and had enough drive and energy to be a leader in the future. Barish is a giant name both on Earth and on the moon," Helms paused then added in a thoughtful and respective tone, "but maybe it's time that Mr. Barish resigns from his position and takes an easy seat as Chairman of the Board and just takes in the profit while his son and daughter work as Chief Executive Officers."

"Michael Barish would make a hell of a good CEO, but Mr. Barish still enjoys the power and the action of running everything," answered Grogan.

"And where does that leave Rachael?" Mulvaina asked.

"Have you ever met Michael or Rachael in any of your work for Barish International?" asked Grogan.

"No, as a matter of fact, I haven't," answered Mulvaina.

"Well, this assignment will take you to the lunar base itself and you will have an opportunity to meet Rachael Barish Farnsworth. She is up there now," said Grogan.

Mulvaina sensed a slightly degrading tone, he thought, in Grogan's voice. It surprised him. He himself was a champion of equal rights and could not dismiss the tone. "She's not a good luck charm, Ted?" Mulvaina sarcastically asked.

Ted Grogan winced and raised his eyebrows, but the facial expression disappeared in an instant. Had he imagined it, Mulvaina wondered, or had he caught a glimpse of a man still harboring in his soul the past centuries old belief that a man had rights over a woman and showed love by keeping her under control even if that meant a periodic abusive hit or two. Mulvaina shook away the repulsive thought. For him, it was too barbaric in this day and age when man commuted back and forth from the Earth to the moon to work, as easily as workers commuted on interstate freeways, to imagine a man holding any old irrelevant cultural beliefs.

CHAPTER 3

The space shuttle glided in darkness seemingly meandering through the stars. Inside the shuttle's passenger seating area thirty passengers occupied forty seats. The passengers looked uniform in their silver coverall garments, almost like plastic figures inside a rocket model, until one abruptly stood up. He was a lean, small man in his early forties. A flight attendant from the back of the shuttle quickly got up and came over to the man.

"Mr. Soots do you need something? Are you experiencing motion sickness?" she asked.

"No, I'm fine, only stretching. How much longer before we land?"

"We are on schedule. We should land in less than two hours."

"I see," said Soots. With his foot he moved the briefcase positioned in front of him and pushed it underneath the seat. "Well, while I'm up I think I'll use the men's room," he said.

The flight attendant smiled and went back to her seat.

Carl Soots advanced slowly down the aisle, his heavy velcro-soled shoes shuffling awkwardly. Self-consciously he glanced at no one. When he reached the restroom door, he scanned up ahead to make sure no one was watching him. Then, he turned to look back and as he did, he saw behind him another door that had been hidden to the main compartment's view due to a dogleg in the corridor. Above this door, painted in bold red letters were the words Authorized Personnel Only. Soots quietly opened the door and entered.

Inside the compartment, against each walled side, were two rows of four self-contained freight pods. The pods were about four feet long, and five feet in height, and three and a half feet in their widest diameter. They were aerodynamically shaped like a space capsule and included a re-entry shield. Off to the side in a heap was a canvas tarp. The floor beneath the pods caught Soots' attention. It was a transport hatch. He assumed it opened so cargo could be released before landing if needed. Soots went to look more closely at one of the pods. He did not see contents marked so he surmised that perhaps the labeling was on the underside of the pod hidden from view. He examined the access hatch at the top of the pod. It did not seem to have a time locking mechanism but an ordinary mechanical latching system. He unlocked it and lifted the pod's lid up and peered inside. Quickly he reached inside his pocket and pulled out a metal vile and began to dip into the pod. Suddenly the sound of footsteps startled him. He felt a shadow. Soots swung around. "Oh…" escaped from under his breath. He quickly regained control then said in an authoritative tone, "I'm just taking a look…" His words were bludgeoned. In explosive pain Soots fell into silence.

Over the shuttle's loud speaker the captain's voice announced, "Will everyone please remain seated and fasten your seat belts for the remaining portion of the flight and re-entry."

Inside the shuttle's passenger compartment twenty-nine passengers sat awaiting their arrival destination.

Inside the cockpit, the captain pushed a button marked with large black letters CARGO DISCHARGE. The shuttle lurched slightly as the pods were jettisoned.

....

Dark clouds were moving fast across the sky. "All hell will break lose soon," said Mulvaina. He looked down at his watch. "Four o'clock. The space shuttle should have already landed. I wonder how long it takes to disembark the passengers. What do you think, Helms?"

"I have no idea," said Helms as he opened the big glass

entrance door to the space port. "This is my first visit out to a space port. Remember I grew up in a small rural town. I just got to L.A. when I started working for you."

"It's only my second trip here actually," said Mulvaina. Then Mulvaina laughed light heartedly and said, "One of my older clients once told me he was interested in flying into space aboard a Russian rocket to the International Space Station. The ticket was a mere twenty million for a one-week stay in space. Of course, that was over twenty years, geez maybe even almost thirty years ago," he said.

Helms let out a long low whistle. "Twenty million for an outer space vacation. Wow!"

"With the discovery of lunar polar water ice on the moon by NASA's Lunar Reconnaissance Orbiter around 2009 and private business getting the presidential push to go into space exploration around 2010," continued Mulvaina, "there was a frenzy to experience space. Space ports sprang up almost overnight in America followed by big cities in all major countries and space tourism took off as a lucrative industry and the hottest 21st century vacation. Of course, most tourists only take a two or three hour suborbital flight and stay for a few nights at orbital cities. But the discovery of water ice was the giant leap for man that put him living and working on the moon."

"The passengers are starting to disembark," Helms suddenly interrupted.

The space port was one large open building, with a single passenger ramp coming, it seemed, right through a wall. Passengers were now descending the ramp quickly and hurrying to the arms of those waiting to greet them. Mulvaina glimpsed a tall man with sandy brown hair walking away alone. He stored the information in the recesses of his mind to be called up if necessary at a future date. He saw a middle-aged couple in tight embrace kissing and crying with happiness. His heart tugged at him with a sad uneasiness. "Scenes like this can really get to a bachelor," Mulvaina said.

"O.K. you can come over to the house for dinner later,"

said Helms. He shifted his position uneasily than asked, "Do you suppose Soots got past us and is already heading down to the baggage area?"

"Possibly. Why don't you go over to the counter and have him paged," Mulvaina said.

Helms walked through the crowd brushing slightly, accidently, against a slender woman who gave him a quick sensuous smile. He felt a warm quiver. Helms inhaled deeply. Just as he knew it would be, he could smell the scent of her perfume lingering. He turned and looked back and got a glimpse of her fading in the crowd. "She has perfect auburn hair," he said under his breath. He turned hurriedly and instantly collided with two heavy-set space port security officers. Half stunned he began blurting out apologies, but impatiently the officers walked briskly by him without words and headed down the entry ramp and straight for the shuttle. Over the tops of heads, Helms spotted Mulvaina waving his hand in a follow-me gesture that indicated Mulvaina was following the security officers into the space shuttle. Helms caught up with Mulvaina just in time so they could enter the shuttle together. As soon as Mulvania saw the flight attendant, her arms tightly crossed and held against her chest and her eyes wide and staring, he knew that whatever disturbance called the security was a thing of the past and was a thing to be reckoned with now.

The captain took the lead and opened the door marked Authorized Personnel Only. Mulvaina flashed his detective license, but no one seemed to be looking. It seemed to Mulvaina that they all had stepped into the compartment at once, as if each were protecting the other from whatever lie waiting inside. At once Mulvaina's eye saw the tip of a boot sticking out from beneath the corner of a heavy brown tarp.

"You said you touched nothing," a security officer said directing his words to the captain.

"As normal procedure, I opened the door to check to see if all pods had been discharged prior to leaving the shuttle. It's part of the post-flight checklist. I never went farther than the door entrance. When I saw that boot like that, well, I went right back to the cockpit and radioed you immediately."

One of the security officers walked over and lifted up the canvas at the opposite end of the boot. "Christ," he blurted out as he threw the tarp back down over the body. When the officer turned around his face told everything, yet he muttered, "crushed skull." Then in a disciplined tone he stated, "Possible homicide."

"Who is it?" asked one of the attendants.

The captain stepped forward and pulled just the corner of the tarp back. "Oh, God! It's Soots. It's Carl Soots, the assistant project manager at the lunar base." He laid the tarp back gently. In shock he rambled, "Maybe he wandered in here accidently and then for some reason didn't go back to his seat when I called for everyone to strap themselves down for the final leg of the trip, then," he paused trying to reason, "somehow, something fell on his head when the pods were jettison and the shuttle lurched away."

"He did get up minutes before the pods were jettison and told me he was going to use the men's room," said an attendant.

"It is either pure naivety or shock that makes such remarks" said one of the security officers. "Don't you see that the poor man was buried in the tarp and his murderer was in such a hurry that he didn't even look back or he would have seen that boot sticking out! Obviously the murderer was trying to get back to his seat and get strapped in before he became conspicuously missing."

The security officer pressed a red button on his two-way transmitter. "Security is now notified to lock down the space port. All entrance and exit doors will be sealed." Turning towards the captain the security officer explained, "Maybe our man is still inside." Then he added in a tone of command, "Captain, we'll also need this compartment sealed off until the crime lab personnel can do their investigation. In case our killer has already left the space port, we'll contact the FBI immediately. Time and crime are intertwined between the Earth and the moon."

Mulvaina made a mental note of the security officer's words. They were well worth remembering. Definitely, Mulvaina reflected, this crime was intertwined between the Earth and the moon. He would have to be an extremely clever observer in both worlds. Of course, he told himself, that was why he was such a successful private detective. He had exceptional powers as an observer that had been recognized by his teachers and even his peers since he was young.   He had also won the school's seventh grade science fair because of his keen observations of the night sky. He had also won a school district-wide writing contest in which he was able to write down a complete physical description of a character in a school murder mystery play and the step-by-step actions of the character during the play scenes. Yes, Mulvaina told himself, he would be an excellent observer in both worlds of this case.

When Mulvaina and Helms were escorted out of the security officers' quarters so they could leave the space port, Mulvaina intuitively knew that there was more to the Barish International investigation then had been honestly discussed at the morning meeting in John Barish's office. He needed quiet time to reflect on the expressions he had seen on Barish's face earlier in the morning. He would talk to Helms about how they were going to handle the investigation while driving back to the office. Perhaps, he thought, they might even finish what they needed to go over in the car and then call it a day by the time they got back to the office. He was thankful he had a week-end to relax, reflect, and make a plan of action before he hit this case. Mulvaina had a feeling in the gut of his stomach that Soots' murder wasn't going to be the only homicide that he would be trying to solve during this case for Mr. Barish.

CHAPTER 4

Seated at an executive desk in a 5th floor private office of the Los Angeles FBI building, George Carver tapped his forefinger repetitively against the cover of a black notebook. "The coroner's report shows that Carl Soots died as a result of a sharp blow to the head," he said. "After Soots was killed the murderer then moved the body under the canvas where it was discovered."

"Do you know where the murder occurred for sure?" asked Robin Mulvaina.

"We're not certain," said Carver, "but we assume it took place in the freight compartment. Some of the expected blood stain patterns were not found probably because they were on the freight pods which were ejected prior to re-entry."

"'I see," said Mulvania. "So you believe the murder occurred before the freight pods were ejected. Have you inspected the freight pods?"

"Only six of the eight pods were recovered, and they shed no additional light on the crime," said Carver.

"Well, why in the hell didn't someone see the body while the pods were being ejected," asked Mulvaina.

"Apparently, the body was well enough hidden under the canvas so no one did. The co-pilot says they only glance briefly at the monitor to see if the pods are ejecting downward."

"And is that flight attendant still sticking to her story that Carl Soots got up to use the bathroom?" asked Mulvaina.

"Yes," said Carver. "Her name is Joan Haney. She's pretty shook up. She wasn't certain about the time, but she definitely recalls that Soots got up to use the bathroom."

"Umm," Mulvaina said in thought. Then he asked, "Do you have any suspects?"

"You know I can't tell you everything, Robin."

"Now, Carver, you know law enforcement is suppose to network with other investigative agencies," Mulvaina said.

"Yes, share information with other law enforcement agencies like local police departments and LEO," Carver answered back quickly.

"Are you suggesting you have suspects listed online. I don't think so," said Mulvaina.

Carver laughed a little. "What am I going to do with you, Mulvaina," he said.

"Listen, George, we've always had a good working relationship and an unwritten mutual support agreement. Have I ever sabotaged one of your investigations? How often have I cooperated with you on my own time? Besides, I'm not asking out of curiosity. I need to better serve my client. Maybe even protect myself."

"I understand, Robin. I'm not trying to put you on hold, or hide anything. I just want you to know that what I'm going to tell you is strictly between you and me for the present time."

"You have my word," said Mulvaina.

"Alright," Carver said. "We're holding a Mr. Gary West in custody. We'll probably charge him tonight. He was a construction worker on the lunar project who was just fired and sent back to Earth. Carl Soots personally fired the man. We've heard that West had threatened Soots' life. I'm leaving on the next shuttle to the moon to personally work on this investigation."

"Guess we'll be seeing a lot of each other then, Carver. I'm leaving on the next shuttle, too," Mulvaina said as he got up to leave. "By the way, I've been trying to locate Soots' briefcase. His widow hasn't received it yet and none of the shuttle people recall picking it up. Have your people got it by any chance?"

Mulvaina noticed that Carver acted surprised by the mention of a briefcase. "I'm afraid not. We haven't seen a briefcase," Carver said.

"I guess that's something you should check online to see if any of your networking agencies are sharing," Mulvaina said.

Mulvaina began to walk out of the room then suddenly turned around. "One thing, George, I want to talk to Mr. West."

"What do you think I am, an interview service? I shouldn't even be telling you that we have West in custody, much less let you talk to him."

"Come on, George, have you so soon forgotten about the warehouse investigation?"

"Which warehouse investigation?"

"The Johnson Electric Company warehouse and John Salvo," answered Mulvaina.

"And so?" asked Carver.

"Remember, you promised me any favor if I would just withhold notifying my client until you had a chance to catch all of the members of the ring in the act," said Mulvaina.

"I believe I said any reasonable request," said Carver.

"This is reasonable," replied Mulvaina.

CHAPTER 5

Dry urine and sweaty arm pits was all Robin Mulvaina could focus on as he was lead to Gary West's jail cell. The stale stench, he thought, could surely be a deterrent in itself, unless of course, you were at the shit level of a rat and thrived in a sewer.

"Mr. Mulvaina to see you," said the guard. The iron bars slid back and Mulvaina looked into the sunken-eyed face of Gary West and his very first feeling was, "This man's not a rat." Mulvaina softened his question, "Why were you dismissed by Carl Soots while you were at Lunar B.C.?"

"Why in the hell should I tell you why I was fired?" West shot back. "I'm not talking to no lousy FBI without my lawyer. Understand."

Mulvaina could feel West's fear through his venomous intonation and see it in West's rolled down slouching and weighty shoulders. Calmly Mulvaina said, "I don't work for the government. I am a private investigator for Barish International. I'm not here to find incriminating evidence against you. I'm here because I've got to find out what happened on board that space shuttle. Somehow you killing Soots, doesn't fit in right now. I've got a gut feeling that you might not have done it, but I can't get to square one if you won't talk to me."

"I'm not a murderer," said West in a voice that was trying to hold back a flood of emotions. "I'm really not. I'm just a lousy s.o.b. drunk. I like to have a few fist fights. I've said insulting crap I latter regretted. But I've never tried to kill anyone. Not even drunk."

"But witnesses claim you threatened to kill Soots when he canned you," said Mulvaina.

"I was drunk when he canned me. That's why he canned

me. I've been canned before for being drunk on a job and I haven't killed any of my bosses yet."

"I saw an FBI report that four years ago you picked a fight with a previous foreman who had fired you a week earlier," continued Mulvaina.

"I was drunk then. It was in a bar and he was a loud-mouthed drunk s.o.b., too. Listen," said West, "I wasn't drunk on the space shuttle. Soots and I never even so much as exchanged glances the whole time. Besides, I was kind of glad he fired me. I wanted to come back to Earth. That place up there is spooky. Nothing's going the way it should. Nothing is ever there on time. Materials are defective. They've got beams that splinter into rubble when they try to pre-stress them. I've worked for a lot of outfits, even for Barish before, and I've never seen a more screwed up mess then the Lunar Base Camp. Hell, I feel bad Soots is dead. I feel really bad he's dead. He didn't deserve what happened to him. He was a decent guy. I might be a mean drunk, but I'm no killer. You hear me. You hear me," said West as he buried his face into his hands.

Mulvaina left the jail convinced West was no killer.

CHAPTER 6

"Thank you. That should do it for today," said Dr. Gray. He walked over to his desk and began writing notes into a journal.

"So what did we find out today?" asked Mulvaina.

Dr. Gray looked up over his wire rimmed spectacles, pinched his lips together for a few seconds in contemplation then stated, "There's a very high correlation between you and Jim here. Seems to be in the range of 75 to 80 percent for demonstrating correctly identification of the card I am holding. The interesting thing is there appears to be some type of color skew, but that's a preliminary observation. We'll have to follow this up on our next session."

"It may be a couple of weeks before we can get together again. I have some out of town business," said Mulvaina.

"Quite far out of town actually," said Helms as he walked suddenly into the room. "Nice to see you again Dr. Gray. I don't mean to be rushing things but, we have a lot to do in a very short time."

"No problem. I appreciate your assistance whenever I can get it," said Dr. Gray.

Mulvaina nodded and then walked over to a young man in his early thirties who was dressed in beige slacks and a beige and orange Hawaiian print shirt. A name tag on his shirt spelled out JIM. Mulvania extended his hand. "Good to see you again, Jim. I'm looking forward to our next meeting."

"Same here, Robin. Take care. We wouldn't want anything to happen to our star subject," said the young man.

Mulvaina laughed. "I'll take good care of myself, don't worry. While I'm out of town I'm going to spend some time looking for the lady on the moon."

"Good for you," said Jim with a wink of the eye.

Mulvaina and Helms walked to the car in silence. They were each thinking their own thoughts about psychic research. As they walked across the parking lot towards the car, Mulvaina suddenly sensed something. It was an instinct being aroused from the deep past of man; a past when man could sense danger just as the deer senses the hunter that has it targeted within the rifle's scope. Mulvaina's vision expanded. He barely heard Helm's mocking words, "Wow! You blew it back there. You had the opportunity to say you were going to be out of this world for a couple of weeks and instead you only said you'll be out of town."

As they approached the car, the car back doors swung open and Mulvaina hastened inside and motioned Helms to do the same. As soon as they were secure into their seat belts, the engine started and the car began to drive away. Mulvaina said to Helms calmly, "Without being too obvious, keep an eye on that blue sedan following us out of the parking lot."

The car headed out on Research Drive and Mulvaina spoke the command, "Keep an even steady 45 mph for about three quarters of a mile until the next major intersection, then make a quick last moment possible left hand turn." Mulvaina looked into his rear view mirror. "Come on. Come on," he said loudly, his words directed to the blue sedan still following them.

Suddenly Mulvaina and Helms felt the car quickly turning left. The blue sedan came around the left sliding over the line divider, rebalanced, and punched the accelerator. "Shit. It's going to kiss our ass," said Helms excitedly. His mind projected the crash and just as he closed his eyes in dread expectation, he heard a familiar siren screaming through the air. He exhaled with relief.

"Slow to thirty," Mulvaina commanded. Then still in a commanding tone added, "Helms, open your eyes and memorize that license plate. I want to know who owns that blue sedan before we leave town."

CHAPTER 7

"Here, Mr. Helms, are some of the biographical reports you asked for," said Gordon Sandusky as he stepped into Mulvaina's office. He walked over to a small conference table where Mulvaina and Helms were seated, pulled out a chair and joined them. "There's some very interesting information on Mr. Barish's daughter, Rachael Farnsworth," Gordon continued.

"Like?" asked Helms.

"Well, for starters, Mrs. Farnsworth was previously married to a Roderick Fellows who was reported to be a rather flamboyant individual; owning expensive cars, considerable gambling habits in Vegas, drinking and carousing all around town. He was reported to have a few steady girlfriends hidden on the side."

"I can always count on you getting the dirt on someone," said Mulvaina. "You should run your own private eye firm not just be my investigative research assistant," Mulvaina continued in a genuine complimentary tone.

"Sounds just like the sort of man Mr. Barish would want as his son-in-law. So how did he get rid of him?" asked Helms somewhat sarcastically.

"It seems that about five years ago, Mr. Fellows tried to fake a burglary attempt on his own house in which his wife, Rachael, was to have been killed," said Gordon.

"I remember it now!" said Mulvaina. "He accidently killed the young woman who was the live-in-maid, didn't he?"

"That is correct and when he realized he had killed the wrong woman, he fled the house," said Gordon.

"I recall the newspaper reports at the time said his wife got a good look at the intruder. She heard commotion, a scream, ran into the room just as the man fled. She, Rachael, identified him as her husband. Wasn't that right?" asked Mulvaina.

"Right," said Gordon. "And," he added, "there was an intense manhunt, but Fellows seemed to just disappear in thin air. The police still have the case open and are actively looking for Roderick Fellows."

"The guy, Fellows, you know, had supposedly gone from bank to bank and drained their savings accounts and also money and gold stashed in safety deposit boxes earlier that day. Several million, at least, if I remember correctly," said Mulvaina.

"Two million six hundred thousand to be precise," quoted Gordon as he looked down at his papers in hand.

Helms let out a low whistle. "That kind of chunk change would easily finance many years of going underground," said Helms.

"Thanks, Gordon. This information is very helpful to have before we head to the moon."

"Excuse me," said a young mid-twentyish girl as she entered the room. "Here is the ownership on that car license you asked me to inquire about." She handed a slip of paper to Mulvaina.

"Quinn Hudson, Private Investigator," said Mulvaina aloud with some surprise. "What in the hell would Quinn's people be doing following us?"

"Got me," said Helms.

"Angela, get Quinn on the phone right away," said Mulvaina irritated.

Soon over the intercom Angela's voice crisply announced, "I have Mr. Quinn's office on the phone."

Mulvaina picked up the phone. "Hello, Quinn. How are you this afternoon? How's business? That's fine. Say, I have a quick question. This afternoon Thomas Helms and I were driving around town and we were followed by two men in a blue sedan license number 5HGF 729. My secretary tells me that the car is registered to your firm. Is this correct? Sure, I can hold for a minute."

Cupping his hand over the mouthpiece Mulvaina looked

across the table at Helms and Gordon. Sarcastically he whispered, "He says he'll have to check."

Mulvaina turned his attention back towards the phone conversation. "Yes, Quinn. That's right. It does. I see. Then could you tell me why you've got men following me? You don't! Well, then, what client have you got those two assigned to…you can't. I really don't appreciate this, Quinn. I don't stick my nose into your business and I expect you not to stick yours into mine. I don't give a shit about your responsibility to your client's interest, you keep your boys away from me or they will end up getting more than a traffic ticket. Have I made myself clear?"

Mulvaina hung the phone up forcefully. "His professional responsibility, my ass!" he said with disgust.

CHAPTER 8

George Carver lifted and let down his heavy velcro-soled shoes purposefully, coming down the aisle slowly, respectfully, almost as if he was walking down a church aisle at a funeral. He reached the third passenger seat from the front, slid into his seat and buckled himself in tight. He looked at Mulvaina relaxed in the seat next to him. "Hell, are you asleep again."

Robin Mulvaina chuckled.

"I'll be damn glad to use a toilet again that has cold running gravity. This weightless crap is for the birds," said Carver.

"I think the seated space toilet is a great improvement. This trip is reminding me of my old Air Force days," said Mulvaina with a smile that eased from the corner of his mouth with happy, youthful memories. "We use to make trans-oceanic ferry flights of fighters behind a tanker. All we had there was a tube at the bottom of the cockpit."

"Not for me," said Carver. "Thank God we'll be there in just a couple of more hours. Three days of floating in my seat is enough for me."

"So what are you going to do first when you get to the lunar base?" Mulvaina asked.

"I'm going to take a real shit," said Carver. Both men laughed. Then Carver asked in a serious tone, "Can you do that on the moon?" Both men broke out laughing loudly.

An attendant passing by stopped and asked, "Is everything alright? Maybe you have that … what's the old expression … cabin fever."

"We're fine. How much longer until we land?" Mulvaina asked.

"It will be just a few more hours now," said the attendant as she gave the men a big public relations smile. Then she added, "Why don't you take a brief nap and I'll wake you when we land." She continued walking down the aisle. Mulvaina noticed that she walked with a rhymatic ease even with her heavy velcro-soled shoes.

"As soon as I can after disembarking and getting checked into lunar lodging, I'm going to interview the crew members of the shuttle run on which Carl Soots was murdered, and everyone at lunar base that knew Carl Soots or even saw him from a distance and recognizes his photo," said Carver.

"Mind if I join you when you interview the crew members of the shuttle run?" asked Mulvaina. Then quickly added, "I haven't had a chance to talk with any of them because they only spent a couple of days on Earth before making a quick flight back."

"Sure, Robin. We should be able to co-operate a lot on our investigation while we're at the lunar base," said Carver.

"Good. Say, are you familiar with the Roderick Fellows murder case?" Mulvaina asked.

"As a matter of fact, yes. I was involved with the interstate manhunt for Mr. Fellows."

"Well, then, what do you think happened to Fellows? Did he skip the country, change identity or what?" asked Mulvania.

Carver thought for a moment. Then he said with honesty, "I really don't know. The maid, a pretty girl, Lucia, was murdered accidently as she was walking down the darken hall from her bedroom to the kitchen. She was forcefully stabbed twice. Once right through the throat and then through her heart. I would really have liked to see that rabid bastard get the death penalty, but we came up with a clean dead end. Of course, with all the money he took off with, Fellows could have done just about anything he wanted to do. Just a few years ago options were wide open to criminals with megabucks in their pockets even with all the robotic eyes watching. Then the Chinese thought they had the loop-hole problems solved when they invented a dark-looking sunglass equipped with facial recognition technology. Our police departments across the country hailed the device as the perfect "catch-all". The sunglasses used the new crystal energy to give them their wireless connection to the police processing station. At the station other officers could see the processing results of the person's true identity and printed out the person's name, gender, ethnicity, and last known three addresses. They could notify the field officer within minutes so they could make a surprise arrest quickly. But the glasses had a short shelf life as a new black market industry to manufacture identities popped-up. Just recently, in fact, we've come across a ring which has been manufacturing new identities for just such clients. The ring has been finding single people, without close relatives and friends, killing them, and then substituting another person, surgically altering the person to resemble the victim. It started years ago, actually, after whole face transplanting became successful. Here was a medical blessing to people who had become terribly disfigured by burns or an accident that has now flipped into evil usage. This is strictly on the q.t. but I have my belief that this is the route our Mr. Fellows took," said Carver.

"So he could be anywhere. Even right under our noses, and we probably wouldn't even suspect him," said Mulvaina more than questioning the idea.

"That's probably right. And as far as probabilities, he might even be working at the lunar base looking for a way to get revenge on his dear ex-father-in-law."

"Interesting probability. You don't actually believe it, do you, George?"

"No, but I thought I might throw it in there to get your uncanny curiosity peeked."

"Thanks. I appreciate the way you describe my intuitive ability," said Mulvaina.

George Carver gave Mulvaina a quizzical look, then pulled his seat belt tighter. "You know, Robin, sixty years ago my grandparents came out to Los Angeles from Alabama on a bus. Five days they spent sitting on hard seats with nothing to do but watch the scenery pass by the window. Now here I am, going to the moon in those same five days. I'm sitting on a rubber-soft seat, quite an improvement, but shit I don't even have any scenery to look at."

"I disagree, George. Space is whatever kind of scenery you make it," answered Mulvaina. "Haven't you ever broken a Chinese cookie and found the fortune that says, Imagination is more important than knowledge."

"Wasn't that Einstein not Confucius?" asked Carver.

"Does truth have a copyright?" Mulvaina fired back. Then added, "Let's think of how an artist can create a masterpiece of landscape within his mind's eye and…"

"Alright, I get the point. Go back to sleep will you. You talk too much sometimes," said Carver.

"I'm already dreaming," answered Mulvania.

CHAPTER 9

At the lunar landing site, the air tower monitored the alignment. The shuttle extended its landing gear that, even without imagination, one might think resembled winter sleds. The shuttle approached the strip and methodically lowered its descent. As it came to the end of the strip, the shuttle suddenly shed its sleds with as much ease as a snake its old skin, extended rubber tires from its belly, and slowed, slowed, until it came to a perfectly smooth stop.

The pilot's voice came over the intercom touched with humor. "Welcome to Lunar Base Camp. It's now just past lunar dawn and the surface temperature is just beginning to inch up some. Remember the moon has extreme temperatures and it is expected to be about 390 degrees Fahrenheit at some point today. Venturing outside you may have difficulty breathing as there is no air, unless, of course, you wear a space suit. By the way, your spacesuit was designed to reflect almost 90 percent of the light that reaches you, so not too much of that heat will transfer to you. Also lucky for you the regolith on the lunar surface doesn't conduct heat well and your boots are well insulated. From the crew of shuttle 504, we thank you for traveling with us and we hope you have an enjoyable stay. We hope you choose SS shuttles for your return flight to Earth which is a winning bet seeing we are the only transportation away from this moonificent place. Well, have a nice visit. You may begin exiting the shuttle now."

Carver was up on his feet seconds before anyone else. "Anxious hey," laughed Mulvaina as he tagged right behind. Just as they passed in front of the cockpit door, it opened and Mulvaina found himself facing eye-to-eye with the five-foot-ten sandy-haired pilot. "Smooth landing," Mulvaina said as he extended his hand.

"You must have been sleeping," laughed the pilot. Then with a smile he continued, "Unfortunately the computer takes most of the credit." The pilot stepped alongside and chatted all the way down the pressurized passenger causeway that connected the shuttle's exit door into the entry hall at the Lunar Base Camp. Waiting in the entry hall was a group of four people all dressed in fashionable business attire. "Well, I must be walking with dignitaries," said the pilot, "because the welcoming party's here." He gave a military-like salute and then departed out the front door.

Carver and Mulvaina were at once deluged with polite but distant gestures of welcome by the group of four. Then, the voices silenced except for one, "Welcome, welcome," said a large boned man with graying hair and a graying moustache in his fifties. "I'm Fred Jones, Project Manager. I hope your trip wasn't too taxing."

"It's nice to be on solid," Carver paused, "moon."

Everyone laughed.

"We all have experienced that sensation of relief as we took the first step onto the moon," said Jones. Then turning towards the others with him he said, "Let me introduce you to the V.I.P.'s. First, the ladies. Without them this new frontier would be unbearable to man." Gesturing in the direction of a tall slender-framed woman, Jones said, "This is Rachael Barish Farnsworth, Vice President of Barish International, next to me is my secretary, Julie Anderson, the most valuable secretary a man could hope for, and this distinguished man is John Farnsworth, President and Chief Chemist for Lunarcrete."

Mulvaina stepped towards Rachael Barish Farnsworth and extended his hand. "Your father just talked to me about you when I met him a few days ago."

"I hope his remarks haven't given you the wrong impression of me. I'm not his helpless little girl." Rachael turned to Carver, "Mr. Carver, how nice it is to see you again."

"It is always a pleasure to see you, Ms. Farnsworth. I only wish that the opportunities of our encounters were not always so tragic," answered Carver.

"Mr. Mulvaina and Mr. Carver," spoke up Julie, "Mr.

Jones has asked that I escort you on a tour of Lunar B.C. prior to showing you to your living quarters."

"That would be very nice of you, Ms. Anderson," said Mulvaina.

"Please, call me Julie."

"Alright, Julie," said Carver. "I wonder perhaps if before we get shown to our quarters, we might first also have an opportunity to talk with the crew of the next departing shuttle. They were the crew members of the shuttle involving the murder of Mr. Soots."

"We have that all arranged," said Fred Jones. "Julie will be taking you to our conference room in about ninety minutes. There are facilities there for you to individually interview the crew."

"Good enough," said Carver.

"Now, gentlemen, if you will follow me," said Julie. She led them out of the entry way and down a long wide corridor with doors numbered alphabetically on either side. "This is our administrative offices corridor," she explained. "Here we have representatives of the sub-contractors, material suppliers, as well as the many federal agencies using the base such as NASA, the Air Force, and the Energy Commission Agency."

"Do you mind," said Mulvaina as he simultaneously opened one of the doors without waiting for Julie's reply. He looked in. "Why I can't believe my eyes. Is that you Joe Grimaldi, old buddy?"

A good looking Italian man with dark black hair and piercing coffee-colored eyes looked up. "Well, you old dog you, Mulvaina. It's about time you came to say hello. How long have you been up here?"

"Just landed this morning. Julie was giving us a guided tour of the base and all my guts just told me to open this door; that inside just waiting for me was either one gorgeous beauty, a hungry tiger, or my old Air Force buddy, Col. Joseph Grimaldi."

"Hey, let's get together as soon as you're settled. Enjoy your tour and your guide. Julie's the real sweetheart of this whole place."

"Compliments will get you nowhere," Julie said with a smile.

"Not so fast, Joe. Let's take a few seconds to talk now. I want to introduce you to George Carver, F.B.I."

Grimaldi got out of his seat and exchanged handshakes with Carver, and then turned and gave an affection man's hug to Mulvaina. "God, it is great seeing you old buddy," he said.

"Sure has been some time. You'll never meet anyone quite like Joe, here" said Mulvaina to George. "Joe and I both served in the Air Force together. He's one hell of a buddy to have when the enemy is attacking."

"Wow! We sure did see a lot of action together, didn't we? So how long do you plan to stay on the moon?"

"Depends on how things add up here and, of course, the shuttle schedule."

"Well, as soon as you're settled let's have a few beers and talk about your detective highlights."

Mulvaina laughed. "Sure thing. Just give me a day or so." Mulvaina watched his old friend walk back to his seat and settle immediately back to work. Something stirred in a dark corner of Mulvaina's brain but he couldn't concentrate enough to see quite what it was. Too foggy. Shuttle lag. He let his focus return to Julie and decided to give the tour all of his attention so he could retain every detail of his new environment.

Julie led them back to an elevator. "We're a little behind schedule but the tour continues," she said with a smile as the elevator door opened. Slowly, the elevator descended. It seemed to Mulvaina it went down about three stories before the doors finally opened to a fluorescent-bright cavernous room. Standing in the middle of the room was a large inflated white plastic-like dome. Its perimeter was anchored securely to a massive concrete footing. Although very dissimilar in most ways, the image still conjured up Mulvaina's memories of childhood visits out to see the historic Goodrich blimp. It use to fascinate him to watch the blimp's huge inflated body struggle for freedom in the currents of the air unaware of its losing battle against the man-made anchors that tied it to earth. Mulvaina remembered the strong impression of how that blimp wanted to rise through the sky and fly. Its spirit had caught his young boy heart and held it captive until he was eighteen and signed up for the Space Force Cadet Program and checked the interest box marked pilot. Suddenly Mulvaina realized his memories had overtaken his presence of the moment and he had walked unaware to the base of the dome. Julie was talking to Carver about some kind of concrete structure that was inside of the dome and was still in its forming stage. Mulvaina was wondering why his mind was drifting so much. He surmised it must be some kind of moon disorientation. He panned his surroundings. The room was full of workmen. Specifically, it looked to him like carpenters, welders, electricians, and masons. He noticed everyone wore yellow hardhats and heavy black work boots. He almost thought he was back on Earth.

One of the yellow hardhats lifted up from a set of blueprints. Julie waved in a "come here" gesture. The man she gestured for handed the plans over to the worker next to him and immediately walked across the room towards them. Watching his stride, Mulvania thought the man's body language conveyed he was someone with some kind of authority.

"Are these our new important guests," the man said with a genuine smile.

"They certainly are," said Julie. "This is Mr. Robin Mulvaina, a private investigator hired by Barish International. This is Mr. George Carver, F.B.I. And this gentleman," Julie paused to catch her breath then continued, "is William Bilks, the lunar base construction foreman."

"Gentlemen, let's not minced words. I know you are here for information so during the rest of the tour, I'll describe as much as time allows. If at any time during your investigation you have specific questions, I'll be happy to answer them for you. We have no deep dark secrets here on the lunar base, although with all the security regulations one might believe we do." Bilks paused. "It was a damn crime what happened to Carl. He was a real likeable guy and did his job well. He wasn't real sociable. Was quiet in the after work hours. I think he spent a lot of time writing letters home to his wife. He was one of those 'one girl only' types. Everyone here was shocked, not only that he was murdered, but that Gary West killed him."

Mulvaina interrupted. "Mr. West is innocent until proven guilty. He's still waiting on the court calendar to go to trial."

"I didn't mean anything by it. It was… I guess, not the way to word it. After all, everyone pretty much likes West, too," Bilks paused for a few brief seconds then continued, "but he has quite a drinking problem. I guess he's an outright alcoholic and that is a danger in the construction field. To be truthful he's a mean drunk. He likes to pick fights with the other men. Has some history, too. I heard he told a waitress that as a kid he beat up his mother while drunk and had been sent to a youth detention camp. Funny thing about West, though, he wasn't brave when he was sober. He would probably piss in his pants if anyone wanted him to fight when he was sober."

"Almost a bipolar personality," interjected Julie.

"Well, let's get back to the tour," said Bilks. "This is the main construction area that you are presently standing in. If you will follow me, we'll enter the dome."

Bilks led the group to a side entrance door and went in first. He walked to the far left side. "Standing here you get a good overview of the inside. The entire site is covered by a high strength, coated fabric that is reinforced, polyvinyl membrane. The membrane is inflated, much like a balloon, and is attached only at the perimeter. The inflated structure provides us with a shirt-sleeve working environment nearly one thousand feet in diameter and one hundred feet high at its highest point."

"How do you prevent any leaks?" asked Mulvaina.

"We have a constant leak maintenance operation. See over there," said Bilks. He pointed to two men working from a mobile extendable arm up near the ceiling of the work site. "One man is holding what looks like a spray gun. He's spraying gas at the ceiling overhead. The outside surface of the membrane has ionized gas sensors. The men spray the surface with a special ionized gas mixture which if any leaks to the outside, they get an immediate reading on the gage to the sensors, thereby telling them they have found a leak. It's really a remarkable and dependable system."

"The construction for the permanent base, well, it looks much like normal construction back on Earth," commented Carver.

Bilks smiled and nodded in agreement. "The permanent structures are being built of a type of pre-stressed concrete, in fact, the high strength pre-stressing cables are shipped up from Earth. However, I proudly say the concrete is all made from lunar material," said Bilks.

"In fact," said Julie, "the lunarcrete is designed and manufactured by the Lunarcrete Company of which Mr. Farnsworth is the president and chief chemist. We'll be visiting his laboratory very shortly."

"Do you mind if I poke around some while I'm here?" asked Mulvaina. And then he added, "Construction fascinates me."

"I think we can take a quick break here, grab a coffee from a dispenser and wait for you," said Julie.

"Alright then take five or ten minutes. Feel free. However," advised Bilks, "let me grab you a yellow hardhat and please I must insist you keep it on at all times Mr. Mulvaina."

Mulvaina thanked Bilks as he put on the hardhat. Then he walked away towards some scaffolding near a partially finished wall. He stopped and began to look closely at the wall's lunarcrete material. He had it seemed only been there a minute when he suddenly felt danger even before he heard a creaking noise overhead.

"Heads up!" came a loud screaming shout from a construction worker.

Mulvaina jumped several feet back in a flash of a second and just in time to avoid being hit by several sheets of plywood-type material. "Sorry mister," hollered the construction worker up above. "You should be more careful walking around here."

"Thanks for the educational demonstration," said Mulvaina

with a sarcasm that escaped his lips unintentionally. He regretted his words the second they were spoken and he pretended not to see the "fuck you" that the construction worker spontaneously fingered at him. At that moment Mulvaina realized he would not be treated with tender gloves just because he was a guest on Lunar B.C.

Mulvaina walked further into the construction site. He stopped near three carpenters working on the ground who were pounding together some forming material. "That's quite something there that you are putting together," he said.

"Yeah, it's forming for a pier and cantilever going in at the second level," said one of them.

"Who are you? One of the engineers?" a tall hefty worker asked in what Mulvaina thought was a sort of mocking tone.

"No. Why?" answered Mulvaina.

"Just wondering. Like to talk to whoever designed this place. These specs are calling for a lot of unnecessary forming. Or so it seems to me."

The last of the three workers made a low howling laugh that was mixed with ridicule and yet some envy. "Yeah, Jeff, maybe you want to be an engineer, right?"

All three men laughed. "How do you guys like living up here?" asked Mulvaina.

A worker looked straight up at Mulvaina. Mulvaina could see the name tag, "Jeff," across his shirt. "It's o.k. I guess. Pays good. Food is lousy. You going to be here long, mister?"

"Mulvaina. Robin Mulvaina. I'm here for just a few days, I hope. I hear that most of the construction workers up here on the moon are non-union people. Does that cause much dissatisfaction towards management?" asked Mulvania.

All three workers stopped what they were doing and turned their attention towards Mulvaina. Jeff spoke again. "No, that doesn't cause any problems up here. Right guys? Why do you care? Do you work for a union?"

"No. Not me. Sorry, let me back track. I'm Robin Mulvania and I work for Barish International. Did any one of you guys know Gary West?"

Jeff took off his yellow hardhat and drove his fingers through his Irish red hair. "Sure we know Gary. He's an alright guy. Rumor has it that they're holding him down on Earth for the murder of Carl Soots. True? What are you digging for?"

"Just need some information." Mulvaina looked down at his watch. "It's later than I realized. Nice talking to you. I'll catch up with you guys a little latter. I've got to get back to the tour Julie is giving of the base."

"Sure," said Jeff. He put his hardhat back on. As Mulvaina began to walk away Jeff hollered, "Be careful, Mr. Mulvaina. I saw you almost get clobbered by the falling forming sheet. A guy could get real hurt up here if he walks around day dreaming and not being careful."

"I'm beginning to understand that," said Mulvaina. He turned and headed back to where Julie and the others were waiting. He did not see but sensed that several other workers left their stations and joined the men whom he had just left.

About forty some feet before being back to where Julie was waiting, Mulvaina caught a glimpse of a slender man, with long blond hair hanging down past his yellow hard hat, who was working diligently on a forming beam.

"Hello there. Is this about where the beam broke last month?" asked Mulvaina.

"What?" hollered down the construction worker.

"I said, is this where the beam broke last month?" Mulvaina could feel the worker looking right through him estimating the effect of talking to him. It calculated out good. The lanky blond man began climbing down the scaffolding. Mulvaina met him at the bottom rung.

"You mean the beam that collapsed when they began to pull the cables," the worker stated rather then asked.

"I guess that's the very one," replied Mulvaina.

"Yeah, this is where it was," the man answered.

"What's the reason it failed?" asked Mulvaina.

"Bad concrete. Well, shit I mean lunarcrete. When they started to pull the cables a pocket of bad lunarcrete crumbled.

They had to tear the whole damn thing out."

"Does that kind of thing happen very often up here?" Mulvaina asked.

"It happens some."

"Does it happen more often than it should?" Mulvaina noticed the man looked slightly to his left and then noticed nervousness when he spoke next.

"Listen, I don't know mister. I'm just a worker here." And the man turned and began climbing again up the scaffolding, but not before Mulvaina committed to memory the name "Russ" written on his nametag.

Mulvaina turned around and found he was surrounded on all sides by four men from the construction crew. He considered the situation quickly. He observed a pile of forming materials a few feet in front of him. He reached into his pocket and removed a small canister and began to walk towards the pile of materials.

"Hey," said one of the construction workers in a demanding tone, "I want to talk to you, mister."

Mulvaina turned and faced the men. "Can I help you?"

A squat heavy-set man mumbled with malice, "No, but we're going to help you."

Mulvaina extended his right arm so that the canister was partially revealed. Slowly he pronounced his response, "Is that right."

One of the construction workers took a hostile step towards Mulvaina. Mulvaina instantly extended his right arm and aimed the canister at the man. "If you want trouble, take one more step and you'll find it," Mulvaina said.

The squat heavy-set man hollered, "Watch it, Sam. I've been sprayed with that shit gas once before and it's no fun. It is worse than a bullet."

"You better listen to your friend. He's got good advice," Mulvaina said.

The worker stepped back. "I've got some advice for you, mister. We don't like people poking their noses into our work, asking questions about union membership and job accidents. You might get some people around here real upset asking foolish questions like that.”

“People like Barish?” asked Mulvaina.

“Maybe,” said the worker.

“I work for Barish,” said Mulvaina.

“And how do I know that,” said the worker.

“You’ll have to take my word for it. Or better yet ask Fred Jones or Julie over there. By the way you will have to excuse me. It seems they’re waiting for me.”

The worker retorted, “I’ll check you out, but in the meantime, keep out of our way. We’ve got a building to build here and a schedule to keep.”

Just then Mulvaina saw Julie waving her hand intensely signally for him.   As soon as he caught up with Julie and the others he said, “Sorry for hanging you up. I was just talking to some of the men. Sort of interesting all the concrete, I mean lunarcrete forming beams around here.”

“Sorry to rush you,” said Julie, “but they are ready for you in the conference room.” Then Julie quickly asked, “Has anything been wrong?” as she looked down at the small black canister Mulvaina was still holding in his hand.

“Oh no,” said Mulvaina. “It’s just an old nervous habit.” He raised the canister and squirted some of its contents into his mouth. “Mouth freshener,” he stated.

•••

Mulvaina focused on the décor of the conference room. One wall was embellished with the Barish logo and another wall was covered with the NASA logo. In the far right corner was a large American flag standing tall, waving gently from a soft invisible current of air conditioning.

Carver started the questioning directing his attention to Dave Rodgers, one of the shuttle crew members aboard Carl Soots’ fateful flight back to Earth. "Did you or shuttle crew member, Herb Jackson, notice Carl Soot's body or the pile of tarp in the freight compartment on your monitor as the captain released the pods?"

"I never noticed the tarp. Or body. And Herb never mentioned anything to me."

"And this monitor is in the back galley portion of the shuttle?" Mulvaina asked in somewhat of a statement tone.

"Yes, that is right," answered Dave Rogers.

"So after the captain released the freight pods, you returned to the passenger compartment?" Carver continued questioning.

"That's right," answered Rogers.

"And neither you nor shuttle crew member, Herb Jackson, noticed Carl Soots' body or the pile of canvas in the freight compartment on the monitor as the captain released the pods?" Carver pressed on.

"I never noticed it. And I already told you Herb never mentioned anything to me," answered Rogers raising the volume of his voice slightly.

"Excuse me," interjected Mulvaina. "Did you possibly see a briefcase," he asked.

"A briefcase?" asked Rogers.

"We've been trying to locate Carl Soots' briefcase. It seems to have been misplaced during the flight," said Mulvaina.

"No, I didn't see a briefcase," said Rogers.

"Did you at any time see Carl Soots or Gary West enter the freight compartment?" asked Carver continuing his questioning.

"No. Never," answered Dave Rodgers.

Mulvaina looked down at a page of a report that had been placed on the desk in front of him. He flipped to another page and then another. He wrote something at the top of the fifth page then looked up and said, "Excuse me once again. It says here, Dave, that you were born and raised in California."

"That's right, Glendale."

"You went to Glendale Valley High School and then went to California State University, Long Beach."

"Well, yes. I started through the university's virtual reality campus program, but I didn't study well independently, and besides I wanted the old university atmosphere, so I went on campus the last couple of years," said Dave Rodgers.

"Oh yes, yes. I see that right here on the paper work," said Mulvaina.

"What did you study?" Mulvaina asked.

"What does it matter?" Rogers snapped back.

"Please," said Carver, "just answer Mr. Mulvaina's question."

"Business," said Rodgers. "I majored in Business and later began a Masters in International Business but dropped it about a quarter into the year. I just finished up the year taking miscellaneous courses in Extraterrestrial Enterprises which was the newest thing hitting the university curriculum."

"Ah yes," said Mulvaina with some reminiscing. "I very well understand how pop trends can entice one down a different academic path. Just as I was graduating there was a witchcraft renaissance and everyone suddenly seemed to be changing their minors to Religion which was the department that took "the sixth sense" under its wing. Even the robotic engineers were minoring in "sixth sense" and trying to see if they could incorporate it into the robotics. You know, our cave man ancestors use pre-conscious faculties as a matter of everyday living. But as man began to concentrate more and more upon making his tools, building places of dwelling, his pre-conscious faculties from lack of use became weaker and weaker. Eventually, it seemed only priests, magicians, witches, and young children possessed the ability to use such powers of their mind. I remember I took a course taught by a self-proclaimed witch who explained that witches could indeed fly. She talked a lot about magical flying ointments which gave a man or woman the ability to fly through the air via broomstick or sometimes without. Of course, she went into more historical and scientific depth in her lectures and explained that these ointments possibly contained some kind of alkaloid which when rubbed into a person's skin caused a state of mental confusion whereby the person could feel as if they were flying. She believed herself that witches flew because they knew through the pre-conscious mind the secret of astral travel. I remember she was fascinated with the old American short story writer, Jack London, and his account of Ed Morrell who supposedly was able to astral travel his way out of prison. I swear that witch if she's still alive would sure be surprised to find that ordinary people now fly through the night sky right up to the moon on a silver-lined space shuttle. Well, enough of my reminiscing. I was serious minded, too, and spent a couple of years studying law courses at your same school. Boy, did I love football season there. The spirit was contagious. There sure were some good crosstown matches. I hear some of the teams have robotic players now. I'm not sure it's all fair, if you know what I mean. Did you go to very many of the post victory bon fires for UC Long Beach that they use to have in front of Tommy Trojan and like all of us, have a little too much good old beer?" Mulvaina stopped and hoped his ramblings confused and hooked Dave Rodgers.

"Sure did. Those were the great days," he answsered.

"I thought," said Carver, "Tommy Trojan was the mascot of USC?" Carver looked at Mulvaina with genuine puzzlement.

"Yes, of course. That's what I meant. The victory bon fires at USC. Isn't that what you thought, Dave."

"What?" Dave Rodgers said in a somewhat confused tone. "I guess so. Maybe I wasn't paying enough attention."

"Well, Dave, that's all I wanted to know. Thank you for your time. I don't have any more questions at this time, George."

"Alright. Thank you Mr. Rodgers. You are excused for now. We appreciate your cooperation in this matter," said Carver.

A door shut quietly. Julie was entering the room. "I'm sorry to interrupt, but I was just checking to see if you gentlemen were finished yet with your interviews."

"Just finished," said Mulvaina.

"Good then. Let's continue your tour. I'll show you some more interesting aspects of the lunar station," she said

"That's fine," said Carver.

"I would like to just make a quick phone call to Earth if I can," said Mulvaina.

"You can use the phone in the booth over there." Julie pointed to a small side room off to the left. "Will you need video?" she asked.

"No, voice transmission will be enough," answered Mulvaina. Mulvaina walked into the phone booth and closed the door securely behind him.

••

Thomas Helms was clearing the dining room table. "Cindy, have you finished all the milk you want?" he asked a small blond toddler who was romping on the floor with a slightly larger blond pig-tailed girl about nine years old.

"No milk. Noooo," squealed the little girl.

A phone rang. Once. Twice.

"My hands are soaking wet. Can you get that," hollered a female voice.

"I can't. My hands are full, too," hollered Thomas.

The pig-tailed girl jumped to her feet and ran into the kitchen. The phone rang for the sixth time. She touched the icon of a phone on the computer screen that was hanging on the kitchen wall next to the refrigerator. "Hello, grandma," she said. "Hello, grandpa. Is this you?" she asked.

Mulvaina said a few words. As Thomas Helms walked into the kitchen, his daughter looked up embarrassed and disappointed and said, "Daddy, it's for you. Some man is calling from the moon."

Helms quickly put his handful of dishes on the kitchen counter. He took the receiver. "Hello," he said loudly.

"Thomas. This is Robin. I'm calling from the moon."

"The connection is good. I hear you loud and clear."

"O.K. Listen. Do me a favor. I need you to get me some

information as quickly as possible. I think I've got a lead on the Soots' murder case. Take this down."

"Hold on. I need to get something to write on." Helms opened a kitchen drawer and grabbed a small computerized notebook. "O.K. give me the information." He tapped out the letters onto the screen.

"Do you have it?" asked Mulvaina.

"Yes. Let me repeat. Dave Rodgers, shuttle crew member employed by Lunarcrete. I'll get right on it. I'll try to see if I can have something back to you by tonight."

Helms tapped the phone icon and Mulvaina was once again far away at the moon.

....

"On with the tour," said Julie enthusiastically. "This next area, the gym, you'll find yourself visiting frequently. Maybe even more than once a day. Up here we have to keep ourselves physically fit by daily exercising. I'm not just talking about weight control but the absolute necessity of keeping your muscles from atrophying. Let's take a quick look; it's quite different than the gyms back home."

Julie opened the door and they stepped inside. Mulvaina was surprised to find himself at the center of a gym that was shaped like a large salad bowl. The outer edges of the gym were rotating around them. He was impressed by the view of people jogging horizontally on the outer and upper edges of the gym. Mulvaina started to take a step forward. Julie threw out her arm in front of him stopping him. "Wait. It's like jumping onto a moving train," she said. "Later we'll come down and I'll show you how to get on the ramp which will take you to the outer exercise ring," she added, her voice calming again.

"I'll look forward to it," said Mulvaina realizing that he really meant what he had just said as he smiled at Julie.

They continued walking down a narrow, long corridor quietly for a few minutes and then Julie pointed at a door as she said, "This is Mr. Farnsworth's lunarcrete lab." Julie opened the large steel door to the lab and Mulvaina quickly panned the mammoth lab room as he stepped inside. It was full of lab tables and benches and storage cabinets. In the right corner was a machine with letters labeling it, "Compression Testing Machine", and another near it labeled, "Chemical Analysis Apparatus". In the back center there was a drying oven. On the left side there was a wall of canvas like cabinets labeled files and books stacked on honeycomb-like shelves and in front of the shelves stood three large concrete-like desks with papers strew upon them.

Mulvaina walked over to the compression testing apparatus. A young Asian male lab technician next to the apparatus looked up and said, "Inside is a test cylinder of lunarcrete being loaded to failure. This dial next to the press shows the increasing load being supplied." The technician's English was perfect. He was definitely American with Asian heritage Mulvaina surmised. Mulvaina glanced at the man's name tag "Gan." Yes, Mulvaina thought, translated the word means adventure and this young man working up on the moon had fulfilled his parent's vision of him seeking adventure.

A bell rang from the belly of the apparatus. "Twenty-five thousand pounds. Not too bad. Kind of an uneven break so it could have even been higher," explained the technician.

"That really can put on a squeeze," said Mulvania with fascination.

"We have a million pound capacity with this machine. Up here we sometimes need it," answered the technician.

Julie came walking up from behind Mulvaina. "Mr. Farnsworth's secretary just notified me that he apologizes for running a little behind schedule and he will be with us in about ten minutes. Make yourselves comfortable, but try not to disturb anything. Mr. Farnsworth is extremely sensitive about his things in his lab," she said.

George Carver came walking over from the direction of the

chemical analysis apparatus. "This is quite some set up. Is this all for just the concrete mix?" he asked Julie.

"So I am told," she answered and then added in a secretarial tone, "Mr. Farnsworth will be able to explain it all to you."

Mulvaina meandered over to the what he felt must be Farnsworth's desk. He looked up and saw that Julie was in deep conversation with Carver. He glanced towards the technician and saw his head bowed concentrating still on the compression apparatus. Mulvaina gingerly took his two forefingers and began sifting through the papers on the desk. After a dozen or so papers, something caught his eye. He looked up. Julie and Carver were still preoccupied and so was the lab technician. Mulvaina lifted slightly a paper tucked beneath the pile and read its title. He committed to memory, "Hydrogenization Of Free Protons and Ionized Deutrium and Tritium in Silicate Ores." Mulvaina slipped the paper back under the pile and walked over to the lab technician. "Do you do all of your testing here on the moon?" he asked.

"Only as it relates to the construction work. Our primary responsibility is quality control. We constantly are shipping material from our quarries back to Earth for extensive analysis and mix design."

"Is that the reason for the pods on board the returning shuttle flights?" Mulvaina asked.

"Precisely. We send back pods of essentially lunar dirt. The pods are released from the space shuttle shortly before re-entry," explained the lab technician. He continued, "The pods descend and settle on the California desert near our main design facility."

"Do you ever lose any?" Mulvaina asked.

"As a matter of fact, we do lose around twenty-five percent of our pods. I'd say an average of two per shuttle. But the pods are pretty cheap and we consider the loss rate acceptable. It's just dirt you know. And the pods are biodegradable with water, rain. Also enriched, I believe, with nutrients that are actually nourishing for the earth's soil. The scientist here thought it was a good experiment to see if they could get the earth's desert blooming. After all, if we intend to start growing crops on other planets we better start trying to do so on our own desert. Recycled water is being pumped from the nearest city out to the drop pod area, and then an underground drip system is being used for the plants. First the desert soil needs to be boosted with nutrients for a few years. Then, you'll be reading about cucumbers and tomatoes growing in the Mohave."

"I see," said Mulvaina. "Sounds like everything has been well thought-out and planned."

There was the sound of the lab door closing gently. Julie's voice drifted through the air, "Mr. Farnsworth, do you remember Mr. George Carver?"

Mulvaina looked across the room at a sandy blond-haired man approximately forty-five that wore brown rimmed glasses and a casual California styled shirt. "Excuse me," he said to the lab technician, "I better join the rest of the group. Thank you for the interesting information."

When Mulvaina reached Mr. Farnsworth the introduction and handshakes were quick. Mr. Farnsworth led the group over to a large apparatus consisting of many mirrors spread over almost a thousand square feet which were all aimed at a central conveyor system carrying material to be heated. "This," explained Farnsworth, "is the solar furnace. As the material passes under the concentrated light, it radiates intense white heat. You'll noticed one problem that's not worked out yet is the extent of the out-gasing and dust, but we're working on remedying the problem soon. Would you like to step up to the viewing port and watch the operation?"

Carver and Mulvaina each took a turn looking through the port. "Fascinating," said Carver.

"During peak sunlight hours," continued Farnsworth, "we can produce approximately ten thousand pounds an hour of lunarcrete cement. At present construction rates, we are just managing to keep up with the demand, but when Phase II begins, it is going to be essential that we have our second phase solar furnace system in operation."

"Is there any problem with getting the second phase going?" asked Mulvaina.

"Not if we get sufficient advanced notice so we can get prepared," answered Farnsworth

"How much advanced notice is required?" asked Mulvaina.

"From what I understand, the Phase II contract is due to be approved within the next few weeks. If we are given the go-ahead immediately, we should be in operation in three to four months," answered Farnsworth.

"Do you think you will have all of your quality control problems solved by then," Mulvaina asked watching for Farnsworth's body language. He noticed a stiffening of his shoulders, but before Farnsworth could answer Julie interrupted.

"Excuse me," said Julie. "We need to get going. I told the security people we'd be there at a certain time, and we only have another fifteen minutes to make it."

Farnsworth looked at the digital clock on the wall. "Yes, I need to be going myself. I apologize for being so late, but I had an important phone call from Earth and needed to resolve a small problem immediately. I'll answer more of your questions later." Farnsworth turned and walked out of the room. The others followed him out of the lab.

Julie led them down another long corridor and to the central security station. Inside there were more computer terminals and screens then Mulvaina could ever recall seeing in one place. He observed that one large screen that took up most of the room's front wall was displaying a schematic of many lighted dots, some moving, some stationery. Next to each dot was a printed code composed of letters and symbols.

One of the security guards rose from his station. "Gentlemen, I have been expecting you. We're quite busy tonight so let me get right to some explanations of how things work around here. The Astro Four System has three major elements. The first is a network of detectors built into the original structure. These detectors are just not eye or fingerprint scans; these detectors are so sensitive as to identify body shape, size, weight, even the gait of every individual being monitored. The system recognizes each person individually. In addition, to this advanced robotic detecting system, Astro-Four uses a more simplified system as backup. Each person wears a coded badge with a magnetic imprint which the system can see. If the badge doesn't match up with the personal characteristics, then the person is identified as an intruder."

"That means that a person could not exchange badges with someone else in order to confuse the system?" said Mulvaina.

"That is correct," answered the security guard.

"What happens if I gain say twenty pounds while working up here?" asked Carver.

"Well, that could happen but not too likely because diet intake is closely monitored and everyone gets plenty of exercise. The third major element of the Astro-Four is its ability to sense gradual modifications of a person's identity when there is a physical change like weight gain or loss. It's interesting you asked that because recently we had one of our supervisors return from an extended vacation on Earth during which time he had lost over fifty pounds and the system initially marked him as an intruder and we had to reprogram it to re-identify him. Because he lost the weight when he was away from the system, it didn't recognize him. If the system had been monitoring him here, on the moon, it would have automatically adjusted to the weight change happening on a daily basis," said the security guard.

"Where are we on the screen?" asked Mulvaina.

The security guard pointed to two very separate and distinct dots. "Right here," he said as he pointed at the location.

"I guess you security people know every juicy piece of gossip about everyone working here," said Carver.

"Not really," answered the security guard with a serious tone. "Certain areas, such as the living quarters, are exempt and do not have an active security system. Management feels it would be bad for morale."

"Is there any way at all a person could penetrate the system without being detected or monitored?" asked Mulvaina.

"Not unless the system has been specifically programmed to ignore that person's presence," answered the security guard.

"Are there any persons that the system ignores now?" asked Carver.

"Not that I'm aware of," the security guard said.

"Who has access to the system that could delete a person's presence?" asked Mulvaina.

"Just, I believe, Mr. Barish," said the security guard.

"Just Mr. Barish," Mulvaina repeated.

CHAPTER 10

Robin Mulvaina inhaled the smells of the cafeteria. The potpourri of aromas made his stomach growl loudly.

Carver patted him on the back shoulder and good naturedly laughed. "Hungry enough to eat a bear, ugh," he said.

Julie smiled politely. "The food is much better than you might imagine for institutional style. Our chef studied cooking in Europe and was a master chef at a well-established restaurant in the San Francisco Bay area when he applied for the job here."

"Why would he give up a good position in one of the best places on Earth to live, to be a chef here?" inquired Carver with a tone of surprise.

"I guess for adventure," said Julie. "The moon is the newest frontier to be seen, claimed, and tamed. What people don't realize is that once they arrive, they are very much confined to the lunar base camp complex. There's not much outside exploring or wandering the surface of the moon. I think a lot of people don't really read the scientific information pamphlets put out by the government, NASA and Barish International about the real state of conditions here. They watch old science fiction films about space travel adventures on imaginary planets and somehow they believe they will arrive on the moon and take explorations of their own. They think they will find secret towns with beautiful women just dying to love a real Earth man and make him the king of their world. Or for some, they come thinking they will find a crevice with untold mineral treasure and," she laughed, "I think some come just to get away from their wives or too demanding lovers. Let's face it, the moon is as far from Earth as a person can go at the moment."

Carver and Mulvaina laughed. Mulvaina thought he felt a

sudden rush of excitement flow through his body. He felt his checks blush. He noticed for the first time that Julie had beautiful coffee-colored eyes. He smiled at her and felt a quickening of his pulse as he observed that she took her tongue and lightly licked her upper lip in a slightly nervous woman's gesture.

"If you two gentlemen would like to go grab us a table, I'll hold our place in line, but hurry back because it doesn't take too long to reach the serving area," she said.

"She's feeling something, too," thought Mulvaina. "Well, come on George, let's get that table before my growling stomach makes a scene," Mulvaina said as he tapped the back of Carver's shoulder.

As they began wandering through tables, Mulvaina's attention was drawn to a cluster of photos on the wall to the right of them.

"Just a minute," he said to Carver and took a few steps closer to the wall to observe the photographs. One was a stunning picture labeled "Mount Everest."

"Every astronaut gets out his camera and loves to take many, many pictures," said a man in a friendly manner who was sitting at a nearby table.

Mulvaina turned towards the man and smiled back.

"Astronauts like to document what their home looks like," the man added.

Mulvaina noted the man's emphasis on the word, astronauts, and decided the man must be part of the moon base support system or a construction worker and not part of the flight personnel. Mulvaina also in that brief exchange intuitively recognized the importance of the man saying "document home" instead of Earth. Surely, he thought, the man was homesick. Homesick for Earth.

Mulvaina turned his attention again to the photographs and in a quick glance recognized Africa's Serengeti Plain and a photo of New York under a night sky. What a contrast, he thought.

"Hey." Mulvaina heard Carver's familiar voice. "I'ld say, old man, you are definitely lost in space. Come on, now. I found us a table."

"Fascinating photos," Mulvaina said as he followed Carver. After a few moments of wandering through tables, Carver gestured to his left to a table that seated four but had only one lone man sitting at it. Carver walked with a quicken step over to the table. "I don't believe who I'm seeing. Frank Engle. How are you?"

"Well, I'll be damned," said a short, portly, and slightly bald man as he jumped to his feet and extended his hand to Carver. "What brings you up to the moon, George?"

Lowering his voice Carver said, "I'm here investigating the Carl Soots' murder." Then returning his voice to a normal tone he added, "Frank, let me introduce you to Robin Mulvaina with MPD Associates. Mr. Mulvaina is representing Barish in this investigation."

As the men exchanged handshakes Carver asked, "So what's keeping you so far from the wife and kids, Frank? Are you working on wiring for the lunar bases's new structures? The pay must be great, uh?"

"I'm the solar electrical superintendent for America Solar Moon Power. Our company has the contract for the entire new project. I really hesitated coming and leaving the family behind, but they made me a financial offer that was just too damn good. I consider it a civilian remote tour and when I go back home, me and the wife are going to buy ourselves the most modern house on Earth." Frank lowered his voice, "Who do you think killed Soots?"

In a subdued voice Carver answered, "I can't tell you Frank, but we do have a suspect in custody at present."

"I'd sure have trouble trying to lay a finger on someone for Soots' murder," said Frank.

"Why is that?" asked Mulvaina. "Was Soots well liked?"

"Hell no. He was a lousy son of a bitch," said Frank. "A damn liar, thief, and blackmailer in my estimation. There are dozens of people up here who have reason enough to rejoice at the fact that he's dead. I'd have a hard time deciding who hated him the most. I know I sure did."

"Why?" asked Carver.

"Because he was on the take from all of us," answered Frank.

"What exactly do you mean?" asked Mulvaina. "Did you ever pay Soots any money?"

"Let's put it this way. Every month I submit my monthly billing for time on the job. When I submit the bill, I give Soots a couple of hundred bucks under the table."

"Why?" asked Carver again.

"Because if I didn't the bill just doesn't get processed that month. When it does get processed at last, it comes back with some disputed figures. You resubmit a month later and it still comes back with disputed figures. The third time around, if you're lucky, you get paid, but that's after waiting three months for your paycheck. Do you know what the interest alone on a ten thousand dollar bill over three months would be? That's not even counting the hell of a jam you're in with no money in your pockets and the wife back home having no money to pay bills and a bank threatening foreclosure. It's a hell of a lot cheaper just to hand Soots, or whoever, their couple of hundred bucks," said Frank.

"That's bribery. You could have taken him to court," said Carver emphatically.

"You've been working with the FBI too long old buddy. You think everything is black and white. No sir. There's a lot of fuzzy grey in the world of business not only on Earth but especially up here on the moon. Survival is learning to live in the grey, my friend," said Frank.

"Now that Soots is gone, who's taking the payoffs?" asked Mulvaina.

"I haven't been approached by anyone new yet," answered Frank.

"Well gentlemen, I hope you like my choices for you," said the cool and rather put out voice of Julie as she approached the table carrying a large tray stacked high with food. "Are you men just going to sit there and continue to let me struggle with this tray or help me? I assume chivalry, what's left of it in the human species, you left on Earth."

Mulvaina almost jumped towards Julie in his immediate effort to take the tray from her and place it on the table. "I owe you," he paused and held her eyes with his own for a few seconds then added, "a night out on the town if you'll accept." Mulvaina was immediately surprised by the words that had just come quickly out of his mouth.

Julie laughed good naturedly. The awkward moment of having left her at the cafeteria line was gone. "How far into the future do you intend for this night out to be?" she asked then quickly added with a wink of eye to the others, "it takes time to adjust one's language to moon life. Sort of like how you need to eliminate the phrase "you see" in front of a blind person. There's no town yet. A night out is in the one and only pub in the basement section of Lunar B.C." Julie sat down. "I don't know about the rest of you, but I'm absolutely starved," she said.

"Do you know Frank Engles?" Mulvaina said feeling somewhat aroused as he took the chair to sit next to Julie.

"Of course," said Julie. "Hi, Frank," she said casually, but with a tone that hinted slight dislike. Then, looking at Mulvaina directly she said, "We see Frank very regularly on the last day of the month. He's like perfect clockwork. Frank's very punctual about his billing."

"This food doesn't look so bad," said Carver interrupting Julie purposefully.

"Don't let looks deceive you, George. Living up here long enough, you'll learn to hate the word "freeze dried" with a vengeance," said Frank.

"Amen to that," said Julie as she put a forkful of food into her mouth.

Mulvaina noticed Julie's perfectly shaped lips were a glossy pinky/brown. Sitting next to her, he found himself taking a deep breath to inhale her scent. The sweetness of vanilla. He liked it.

CHAPTER 11

The corridor had the same monotonous gray vinyl floor, but the walls were not painted stark white like the rest of the lunar base complex walls Mulvaina had seen so far. In fact, Julie had to tug on his arm sleeve several times and with a gentle smile prod him along his way, for Mulvaina found the walls lined with moonscape photographs too fascinating to just hurriedly walk past.

"Very artistic work," said Mulvaina. "These walls are certainly not a collection of amateur photographers' work."

"No wonder you are a detective. Nothing seems to escape not only your observation, but also your judgment, Mr. Mulvaina," said Julie. "In fact, all of our living quarters' corridor walls display the original photographic works of Charles York. He is a brilliant young artist that is presently living here on the moon."

"I hope you can arrange to have George and I meet him while we're here. I've always been fascinated by landscape photography. In fact, I have quite a collection of the twentieth century Ansal Adams' work."

"I think that can be arranged. I don't know him well myself," said Julie, "but Mr. Farnsworth does. In fact, I think it was Mr. Farnsworth that arranged for the artist to come up to the moon on some kind of art grant."

"So Mr. Farnsworth is not only a practical scientific person, but also a man that is quite appreciative of the arts," said Carver in a sort of reflective tone.

"Yes, that would begin to describe him," said Julie.

"Begin," said Carver.

"Hmm," said Julie then added, "there's more than meets the surface with Mr. Farnsworth. I guess."

"What do you mean guess?" asked Carver.

"Well, I'm not the kind of personal friend that Mrs. Farnsworth girl-talks to and discusses personal intimacies of her marriage or problems or desires and secrets, but I have heard through friends of mine, that are closer to her, that Mr. Farnsworth is quite the devoted husband and lover."

The corridor filled with an awkward silence and Mulvaina heard the soles of their shoes against the gray vinyl and noticed Julie nervously twisting the small gold loop in her ear.At last Julie, herself, broke the silence. "Here we are. This is your room Mr. Mulvaina and Mr. Carver you will be right across the hall." Julie took a key out from the pocket of her skirt and put it into a key lock at the side of the door. Electronically the door began to slide open.

For just a brief second something gleaming in the unlit room caught Mulvaina's eyes. Spontaneously he grabbed Julie by the arm and threw her sideways while hollering, "George, watch out!" Silently a bullet drove through the air barely missing Mulvania and embedded itself into the frame of the doorway.

Carver and Mulvaina, their backs to the wall, took positions on the opposite sides of the door opening. Carver withdrew a revolver from a hoister strapped to the inside of his jacket. Mulvaina pulled out a small revolver from under his shirt.

"How in the hell did you get that up here?" Carver asked in a second of surprise.

"I'll explain later, but aren't you glad I did," Mulvaina retorted.

Just then Julie let out a brief scream.

Mulvaina's eye caught the movement. "The eleven thirty position. About three meters back. Meter above the floor," he hollered.

Carver took off his shirt and held it in his left hand. "So when I give the word, I'll go high, you low."

In an instant Carver was waving the shirt in front of the door opening and then he threw it inside. A rapid shot penetrated the shirt. Carver and Mulvaina rushed into the doorway and fired, then both men instantaneously and simultaneously dropped down behind furniture.

For a few brief seconds there was nothing but suffocating silence. Then there was a moan from the depths of a man's guts, not unlike the pitiful sound of a wounded elk as it gives up its spirit when the hunter's bullet penetrates its body. The wounded sound filled the dark space of the room. A barely audible muttering, "Hel……..". Then a crash as a body fell hard against the floor.

Mulvaina called out, "Julie, where's the light switch?"

"On the left….left side….of the door." Julie quivering voice strained to be loud.

Mulvaina groped for the switch. When the light went on, the men stared at the body of a man, face down, lying in an oozing stream of blood. He was clothed in black with a head full of curly black hair. His hand had a death grip on an automatic silencer.

Carver cautiously walked over towards the man. He aimed his pistol at the man's head. When he reached him, he slowly lifted his shoulder and rolled him over.

Julie gasped and threw her hands over her face.

"Shit, it's Dave Rodgers," said Carver.

"What the hell? I had this strange feeling about him," said Mulvaina.

"Clue me in on your hunches next time old buddy," said Carver with a tone of nervous relief.

"Listen. Do you hear that hissing sound?" asked Julie.

Sissssssssss. The sound reminded Mulvaina of air escaping from a helium balloon. Sissssssssssss. It hissed with vemonous foreboding.

"Look here," shouted Carver. "It appears a bullet hit the window seal. I must be hallucinating or something because it looks like it's expanding and getting bigger every second."

"Oh my God. We're decompressing. Hurry. Let's get out of here," screamed Julie. She turned and darted towards the door.

Suddenly a loud deafening buzzer filled the room. Instantly, the entrance door slid shut. Carver rushed towards it and began banging it hard with his fists.

Julie reached up to the top of the door to a button panel and pushed a red button labeled emergency in bright red letters. She pushed it again and again and then said in shock, "We're locked in. Locked in." Then her repetitive training in emergency procedures took over her voice. She turned to the men and said, "Stay calm. Be calm. Emergency procedure. Survival Bag. Alright. Look for a box." Julie quickly surveyed the room. In a corner next to a tall coat rack she saw a dark brown chest-like box. She darted over to the box and opened the lid. Julie let out a sigh of relief as she took out a bulky plastic bag which had a small tank attached to it. As she pulled back the bag's zipper, the bag expanded into a huge tent shape. "Here get inside of this bag," Julie said to Carver. "Pull this wire to open the oxygen bottle, then zipper yourself in. The rescue crews will know we're in here and they will get us out as soon as possible. Quick now. There's only seconds." She reached back into the dark brown chest and grabbed another bag and handed it to Mulvaina.

"Same thing," she said quickly. She grabbed up a third bag.

"I seem to be having trouble getting the damn zipper to move!" said Mulvaina somewhat excitedly.

Julie reached over to Mulvaina's bag and tugged hard on the zipper. "What? Someone has sabotaged this bag," she stammered confused, then regaining her procedural confidence said in a monotone, "Here, take the bottle off and clip it to my bag and get inside with me."

Julie started to zip up the bag. About mid-way up it stopped. "Too wide," she mumbled and pressed herself tightly against Mulvaina. She yanked the zipper upwards. The zipper went up and automatically locked.

Julie stuck one bottle's straw like tube in Mulvaina's mouth and the other bottle's straw in hers. Mulvaina could feel the air filling in Julie's breast. He realized his cheek was lying against Julie's cheek out of pure strategic necessity, but still he was surprised to find that now in this time of emergency and possible death, he was beginning to feel aroused. He breathed in the oxygen lightly not knowing how long he might need to rely on it or how much there was in the bottle. He closed his eyes and willed for the rescue crew to come quickly.

If he had ever wondered whether or not he might have any telepathic abilities, Mulvaina suddenly came to believe either coincidence was quite prevalent in his life or he did, for he had just closed his eyes and created and visualized the rescue crew for no more than a brief few minutes when he could hear the entrance door being pushed open and men entering the room.

In seconds Mulvaina felt the tent-like bag being lifted up and then he was in an awkward hanging position. Mulvaina heard a rescuer say, "This one looks dead."

"Throw him on the dolly. We'll let the paramedics make the final call. I'll grab the other Emergency Decompression Survival Bag," said another rescuer.

"So," Mulvaina said to himself, "I'm hanging from a dolly." Suddenly Mulvaina felt himself helplessly moving along in this hanging position that under normal circumstances would have been unnerving, but at this particular moment he was instead distracted with the sensation that the movement seemed to press Julie even more tightly against him.

The dolly seemed to roll down the corridor for endless minutes then suddenly Mulvaina felt an abrupt stop and the bag was being unzipped and someone was taking the straw out of his mouth. He felt disoriented. He could hear sounds but not get the words.

"Mulvaina! Are you o.k.? Hey, man, you're o.k."

"I'm o.k.," Mulvaina finally said.

"What in the hell happened in there?" asked one of the paramedics.

George Carver withdrew his badge from the inside of his shirt pocket. "Take Mr. Rodger's body immediately to the hospital to verify death, please. Don't disturb the body in anyway. I'm taking full authority concerning this matter."

Mulvaina noticed that Carver's hand holding his badge was trembling. He also noticed that Julie was nervously smoothing down the material of her powder-blue skirt. He admitted he, too, felt shaken.

"Damn, I guess we're lucky those emergency bags were in the room," said Carver.

"Actually," added Mulvaina, "we are lucky Julie was with us and knew about the bags in the room."

"Has nothing to do with luck. In fact, in my opinion, everything about what just happened was sort of unlucky!" said Julie. "I am required to brief you on the Eddysub Bags when you first arrived at the base, but since you had to rush to interview the shuttle crew, I decided to wait until we got to your rooms. I broke one of the top safety rules and it could have cost you your lives."

"Talking about our lives," Carver paused for a few brief seconds then said, "what's your idea Mulvaina on why Dave Rodgers wanted to end ours?"

CHAPTER 12

Shuttle lag, the tour, interviewing, and an episode of near death were all catching up at once on Mulvaina. He yawned widely. Once. Twice. Again a third time. He stretched out on an army like cot and closed his eyes. Julie had repeatedly apologized for the breach of security and her inexcusable breakage of the safety rules, and then, for the total unavailability of another private room and thus the inconvenience and necessity of Mulvaina and Carver now having to share a room. Mulvaina found some comic relief in the fact that he was lying on a flimsy cot instead of the room's twin bed because, at the flip of a coin, he had chosen heads instead of tails. "Oh well," he said under his breath, "What did it really matter. At least he wasn't laying stretched out dead in a cardboard casket." He yawned again and sat up on the edge of the cot not wanting to allow himself to fall asleep. He looked at his watch, a digital 24 hour watch set on Pacific Standard Time; the watch his mother had given him for his thirty-fifth birthday. It was already half-past nine.

Mulvaina got up and went over to where a bright yellow phone hung magnetically from a silver strip on the wall. He picked it up and began talking, "Hello, operator, can you please call the following Earth number," he said awkwardly. The connection was remarkably good Mulvaina admitted to himself as he heard Thomas Helms answer the phone with a normal toned hello.

"Glad to hear your voice. I mean your voice is real clear," Mulvaina said.

"Yea, I can hear you loud and clear, too," said Helms. "Listen Robin, I've got some information on Dave Rodgers for you. I got it directly from the central information system's file. It reads pretty straight. Dave Rodgers is a college graduate. Steady employee. Most of his family has passed away. He lives by himself. Has a few, not-too-close friends, but sort of a loner... . He what? Are you o.k.? Thank God. What about Rodgers? Dead! Carver is, I assume, running a complete FBI identity check. Yes, I'll keep on it. Also, I'll let you know if I come up with anything. Say Robin, there is some additional information I would like you to get while you're up there. Could you get the records of materials ordered, delivered and lost."

"Right," answered Mulvaina. "I can probably get those files from Jones' secretary. Anything looking irregular?"

"Well, it's interesting that ten suppliers seem to account for the vast majority of the lost or damaged shipments. What's even more interesting to me is that six of these companies are all subsidiaries of the same parent company. And get this for a final point of interest, the principal owner of the company, Harry Sellers, was a fraternity brother in college with Fred Jones and no other than Mr. Roderick Fellows. But don't let all this keep you awake. Get some sleep, Robin," said Helms with sincerity.

"Harry Sellers, Fred Jones, Roderick Fellows," Mulvaina repeated several times until he succumbed to sleep that turned into only a quick nap when a loud rapping at the door woke him.

CHAPTER 13

Dance music was playing loudly from a small-sized robotic band tucked into a corner of the basement bar room. Tables were jammed into the room so tightly that Mulvaina could feel his shoulders rubbing against someone else's shoulder every time he shifted in his seat. "He was really too tired for this kind of socializing tonight," he had said, but he had been unsuccessful at persuading his old buddy, Joe Grimaldi of this fact when he had come knocking at his living quarters telling him he had heard about his narrow escape from death and that he wanted to buy him a beer and show him some moon hospitality.

So Mulvaina tried to get his second wind, which was so easy in youth and getting to be a harder feat each year. "How's the family?" Mulvaina asked after a few long sips of his beer.

"Dolly's fine. The kids are almost grown. The oldest is in college. How about you? Did you ever settle down with that brunette?" Joe asked.

Mulvaina shook his head. "Ever since I broke up with Ellen, I haven't really found anyone I could develop a meaningful relationship with. And, I've been damn busy getting and keeping my business going. After today especially, I am convinced the investigation business is a lousy profession to ask a wife and family to endure."

"As bad as the military?" Joe asked but really was making a statement of fact.

"Yeah, really. So how do you like being assigned to NASA?"

"It's like being in the Air Force. Up here my job is purely administrative. I oversee NASA's interests and make sure Barish is doing things according to specifications. I have a good staff working with me," said Joe Girmaldi.

"Are you familiar with the contract being negotiated for Phase II?" asked Mulvaina.

"Sure. I helped write part of it," answered Joe.

"On a project like this, how are the subcontractors protected in the contract?"

"How do you mean, Mulvaina?"

"Well, for instance, take Lunarcrete. Here they need a much larger solar furnace and a reliable supply of raw materials for the concrete-like mix."

Girmaldi interrupted, "As a matter of fact, Lunarcrete, unlike many subcontractors, is directly written into the contract with certain specific rights, privileges, and responsibilities. For example, "Lunarcrete has the right to build an enlarged solar furnace with all the necessary support equipment and necessary manufacturing equipment. Lunarcrete has the right, in fact, to quarry for raw material anywhere within a hundred miles of the Lunar Base Camp and the company even maintains a twenty year exclusive privilege to operate its quarries."

"Interesting indeed," said Mulvaina. "And what if they were to find something in the quarries not related to concrete, but which was very valuable, say like gold?"

"Unlikely, old man. But if they did, the company would according to contract have a twenty year exclusive right to mine it," said Girmaldi.

"Wow!" said Mulvaina. He looked up to signal the waitress for another beer and saw Julie just entering the bar. He waved her over and jumped to his feet pulling out a chair for her as she approached their table.

"What will you have?" he asked.

"A beer's o.k," Julie answered with a smile. "Hi, Joe." She glanced around the bar.

"And where is Mr. Carver?" she asked.

"He's still tied up I guess with the Dave Rodgers incident; but I can manage the party without him." Mulvaina smiled at Julie and wondered if his flirtatious remark seemed too boyish. He felt a little awkward suddenly.

Julie and Joe seemed to save the hour or so that passed talking shop and filling Mulvaina in with details of lunar base life; its ups and downs and moments of pure comic relief. It seemed to Mulvaina very much like life on Earth. Suddenly and without warning Mulvaina yawned widely. "Excuse me. It's been quite a day," he said rather embarrassed.

"I think it's time to call it a night. Come on. I'll walk you back to your room so you don't get lost," said Julie with a smile.

Mulvaina smiled at Joe and reached out and shook his hand. "See you later old buddy." Then turning to Julie, Mulvaina said, "Lead on."

Of course, Mulvaina surmised, it could be his imagination, but he felt Julie was walking very slowly down the corridor as if in some female gesture she was trying to make the evening stretch out and last. He liked the thought. "Do you find it boring confined to the moon? I mean, being at the same place, day after day, week after week?" he asked only for conversation sake.

"Looking at the same walls and breathing the same air with the same people can start to get on my nerves when I'm tired, but on the whole my work is interesting. I feel part of something important, something in fact, incredibly monumental." Julie suddenly grabbed Mulvaina's hand. "Come with me. I want to show you something," she said with schoolgirl enthusiasm.

Julie quickened her pace and soon made a sharp turn left down the corridor and when they came to the end of it, almost tucked into the wall was a flight of narrow steps. She raced up the stairs until they dead-ended into a door. She pushed a button and the door slid open. Smiling, she yanked Mulvaina inside.

The lights were off, but as soon as his eyes adjusted, Mulvaina saw small scattering star-shaped lights forming a path through the room. Julie took his hand leading him through the path to the center of the room. Mulvaina quickly estimated he was standing beneath an approximate twelve foot diameter hemispherical clear dome.

"They use this room as an observation center and as an

observatory. This time of night, it doesn't get much use," said Julie.

Julie led Mulvaina up the steps to the platform. "Take a first look," Julie whispered.

What Mulvaina saw took his breath away. "Wow, how fantastic. The Earth appears so large," he uttered.

"It's so beautiful." whispered Julie.

"Like you," Mulvaina heard himself say as he gently leaned towards Julie and kissed her. Mulvaina was taken by surprise as Julie threw her arms around his neck and kissed him with an abandoned intensity.

Suddenly the moment and silence of the room was broken by the sound of the door sliding open and footsteps entering. Julie pulled herself away from their embrace.

Somewhat sheepishly, George Carver walked up to the bottom of the platform. "Security told me I would find you here," he said.

"Come on up, George. There's a panoramic view that's unbelievable."

"Come on up and have a look," beckoned Julie.

"I would love to, but I'll have to pass for now. Robin I need to talk to you. It's rather important," Carver said in a serious and urgent tone.

"I better let you two be alone then," Julie said. She took Mulvaina by the hand and lead him down the platform steps. When they were at the bottom Julie smiled and said, "Thank you, Robin for the drink and company. See you tomorrow. Good night, Mr. Carver." Then she walked quickly out of the room without turning back.

"Sorry to interrupt," said Carver. "I just got back the confirmation on the fingerprints I sent of our gunman. The prints, it is believed by our Homeland Security experts are not really Dave Rogers. The finger tips have been surgically altered, but scan as Dave's. Analysis of deeper tissue levels reveal them to be those of Aldo Rotacello, a notorious mob enforcer, who was convicted and sent to death row for kidnap and murder three years ago. It seems he managed to escape while being transported to another trial he had promised to testify as a witness in, and the police never found him."

"Are you sure it's Rotacello?" asked Mulvaina surprised.

"Here's your answer to that question, Mulvaina. Rotacello closely resembles the photos of Dave Rodgers. However, our man's dental work matches with Rotacello's and he has a bullet scar on his back which matches with the description of the one Rotacello had received. Add another interesting point. Our gunman has, not aging wrinkles, but fine facial scars indicating he has undergone intensive facial plastic surgery."

"And the real Dave Rodgers lived alone and had no close family or friends," added Mulvaina.

"You guessed it," said Carver. "Listen, why don't you go back to the room and get some sleep. I've got a couple of more leads I want to try to nail down then I'll be right along. I have a feeling that we may have to extend our moon reservations. There may be more than meets the eye up here. I've heard you have some strong intuition. I sure in the hell hope so, because I think we're going to need some basic human instincts to deal with all the scientific wizardry that is going to come up against us here."

CHAPTER 14

Mulvaina yawned without restraint as he opened the door of his living quarters. Fatigued, he half stumbled into the room and didn't notice for a couple of seconds that the lights were fully on. He swung around and found a woman, her long black hair flowing down the back of her shoulders, seated on his cot. "Oh. I'm really sorry. Excuse me. I must have the wrong room," he said terribly embarrassed.

The woman stood up and turned towards him. "Mrs. Farnsworth," Mulvaina said in surprised recognition.

"Mrs. sometimes makes me feel so old. Call me Rachael. I didn't want to ask you today in front of the others, but I was curious about how long you have been working for my father because I've never heard your name mentioned in conversation."

"About four years now. My firm has been involved in investigating several fraud cases within your company and also an internal security problem."

"Do you enjoy your work, Robin?"

"It's like any other job. It has it's good and bad days."

"Are all days as dangerously bad as today? I really must apologize profusely for the failure of our security system. You see we try to protect a person's privacy while in living quarters, but as in the case of today, that protection has its definite limitations."

"Along with freedom there are always risks," answered Mulvaina.

"At least one thing positive resulted from today's unfortunate incident," continued Rachel.

"That is?" asked Mulvaina.

"With the unfortunate shooting incident at least you have wrapped up the Soots' murder case," Rachel said with a tone of relief.

"It does appear that way doesn't it, but that's not the only reason I was sent up here by your father," Mulvaina said directly watching Rachel's facial expressions.

"Barish International is very important to me," Rachel said without emotion in her voice. Then she continued, "If you explain to me what else it is you need to find out, I'll be happy to help you in whatever way I can. I have always tried to be a very loyal daughter. I mean in every aspect. My father has eliminated filling me in about your purpose; I assume for the same old reason that somehow he still thinks of me as his little girl instead of an intelligent and capable woman. Maybe he felt he was protecting me."

"Protecting you?" inquired Mulvaina.

"Well, ever since Carl Soots' murder I have felt very uneasy up here. I probably have conveyed my anxiety when I have spoken to my father," she said.

"Oh, he's come up to the moon since the murder then?"

"No. He's wanted to, but he has been too busy with the new contract negotiations that he hasn't had the opportunity, and then also, he's been quite sick. It's an old stomach condition. I meant when I had spoken to him on the phone. I talk to him quite frequently. Sometimes daily."

"Oh I see," said Mulvaina. He was listening very carefully to Rachael's intonations of each word. Something in her talking was perking up his interest. He didn't know quite what it was. It would come to him in time.

"Well, at any rate, John is a well meaning man, but he has not been able to give me a real sense of security. He's brilliant, you know. But so academic. He lacks that tough-guy instinct my father has, and that I guess the woman part of me needs. You seem to have that macho-type personality, Robin. In fact, you seem less unnerved tonight than John after one of his lunarcrete stress tests fail."

Mulvaina heard her discontent. He needed more information to get to know her under the skin. He softened up his questioning and mixed it with personal talk. "I've learned to cover up my feelings pretty well. I mean in this business, it's a matter of survival. I come across a lot of danger and well, I just can't be as they say, an open book. You can't ever let the other guy know when you're scared, or you've lost your advantage and sometimes just lost completely. Do you understand?"

"Completely. I'll keep that bit of advice. It'll probably come in handy sometime. Now it is late. Before I leave, are you sure there isn't any information I can give you that will give you a head start in your work for tomorrow?" Rachel asked again.

"I was wondering if you think your first husband, Roderick Fellows, might be up here?" Mulvaina asked with no emotion in his voice, and carefully watched Rachel's facial expression.

He instantly noticed that Rachael seemed to gasp just slightly under her breath and her eyes widen.

"Here? On the moon?" she asked truly surprised by Mulvaina's question.

Mulvaina nodded affirmatively.

"Preposterous idea!"

"Can you be so certain?" Mulvaina questioned with a little push. He focused his attention on her body language for any suggestive clue.

"Of course. I would spot him in a second. Everyone here has a specific job. I mean there is no place to hide on the moon."

Mulvaina noticed Rachel's index fingertip reached up and touched the corner of her mouth. "I don't mean to alarm you," he said "but the man who was shot in my room today was not who he said he was."

"What do you mean? What are you trying to say Mr. Mulvaina. Are you saying that Dave Rodgers wasn't Dave?" asked Rachael in a confused tone.

"He was an imposter," Mulvaina simply stated.

"What are you talking about?" replied Rachel raising the tone of her voice a little.

"The man who shot at me was a convicted mob enforcer who broke out of prison some time ago," Mulvaina said without any emotion.

"Oh my God! Does my husband know this yet?" Rachel said with some nervous excitement.

"I'm not sure. George Carver just received the information a little time ago. I'm sure if he didn't think it was too late he might have already discussed it with him, otherwise, he will do so first thing in the morning," said Mulvaina as a matter of fact.

"I see," said Rachel.

"Getting back to your first husband…"

Rachel interrupted, "Yes, go on."

"I suspect he may have changed his identity. I mean his appearance. He could be anywhere, perhaps even here on the moon," Mulvaina continued.

Rachel suddenly stood up. "Now that's getting a little far-fetched Mr. Mulvaina. The personnel here are too well screened."

"Are they? Then can you explain how someone managed to impersonate Dave Rodgers successfully? Your first husband could be anywhere, perhaps as a workman or electrician."

"Roderick would be incapable of impersonating a workman or any kind of skilled craftsman. He could never do a simple handyman chore around the house. In fact, he could never do an honest day's work if his very life depended on it. All that man was good for was drinking, gambling, and carousing with low class women. We have no positions on the moon for those kinds of qualifications."

Mulvaina not only heard her discontent once again but also observed the anger not only in Rachael's voice but also in her eyes. He knew to prod and question more. "But there is always a possibility," he continued, "a possibility, and only you might be able to detect some slight tell-tale trait which he has not been clever enough to mask."

"It's late. I really must be going. John will start worrying where I am," said Rachel obviously upset with Mulvaina's continuing prodding and questioning.

"Certainly," said Mulvaina a little surprised at Rachael's abrupt closure of their discussion and lack of offer for assistance.

He quickly added pushing for a response, "Will you help me if I come upon a person of interest? For that tell-tale sign only you could see?"

Rachel replied changing the subject, "I understand my husband, John, is taking you on a tour of the quarries tomorrow."

"That's correct," said Mulvaina noticing that Rachael had deliberately stressed the words, 'my husband, John'.

"Well, you'll need a good night's sleep so you are alert tomorrow and don't miss any of the fascinating details of the moonscape," said Rachael in an almost chilling tone. Then, she simply turned and walked out of the room.

CHAPTER 15

"Good morning gentlemen. I am Rasahiko," said a stocky, young Oriental man dressed in loose brown clothes, his shinning black hair pulled tightly back away from the sides of his face.

Carver and Mulvaina walked cautiously into the large room designated EMUA, Extra-vehicular Mobility Unit Area. Every room now was suspect for ambush Carver had told Mulvaina early in the morning when they had only a quick cup of coffee to start their day.

Mulvaina panned row after row of racks hanging with bulky space suits, helmets and other paraphernalia. Did any one of those suits suspended so ghost-like move just ever so slightly? Was there anyone hiding in the shadowy corners? He relied on his intuition. He felt no alarm.

Rasahiko cleared his throat and said, "I'm here to instruct you in the proper method of getting dress for your lunar excursions. Since you're going out to the quarry this morning with Mr. Farnsworth, this lesson will also prepare you for your trip." Rasahiko continued without expression, "You must always remember that the lunar environment is hostile to man. It is not just simply that it lacks oxygen and water. There are hazardous micrometeoroids and space radiation darting around constantly. Without atmospheric pressure, exposed human body fluids will boil. Dressing slowly and conscientiously is always a matter of immediate life and death. You must always have your mind on the location of each important tube being careful not to damage it by rough or quick handling of your space suit."

Mulvaina felt himself inadvertently shifting his body posture into a military like stance of attention.

"On the racks you will observe," said Rasahiko, "three

articles of clothing grouped together to form one unit." He lifted one hanger from the rack. "Think of this piece as water-cooled underwear and treat it with absolute respect. It is your link to a vital backpack, PLSS, Portable Life Support System, where your water and oxygen are stored."

Mulvaina noticed that Carver kept licking his lips in a repetitive motion. He's nervous about something other than this space suit business, thought Mulvaina. He took a deep breath and concentrated harder on Rasahiko.

"Now if you will carefully step into this," said Rasahiko holding the piece of clothing in position and grasping Mulvaina's forearm as he began to step into it.

The meshy fabric, interwoven with flexible tubes, felt odd yet cool against his body Mulvaina thought. He refocused. He concentrated on what the young Rasahiko was saying.

"Over this, you will wear this next article of clothing," Rasahiko was saying as he took down a second hanger from the rack. This piece is made up of numerous diverse fabrics and rubbers and is the assembly that retains the oxygen atmosphere. It, too, is linked into PLSS. Here on the top is a remote control unit that will allow you to adjust oxygen flow and cooling temperature that is personally comfortable."

"How long will the PLSS sustain activity?" asked Carver.

"Up to ten hours. It has been developed to insure a worker can get to the quarry area, work eight hours, and get back to Lunar B.C. before recharging," answered Rasahiko.

"What if something goes wrong in the time frame of the job? Like say, the transport tram breaks down or something?" asked Carver.

"There's a separate oxygen system at the very top of the PLSS that is specifically for emergencies. It has up to ninety minutes worth of oxygen depending on the draw-off rate," replied Rasahiko.

"Boy, it must take some getting use to working in this outfit," said Mulvaina as he rotated his shoulders uncomfortably.

"You're not complete yet," said Rasahiko. "Here's your

armor. This outer coat shields you from the micrometeoroids, ultraviolet rays, and other known and unknow forms of radiation. And here's arm bands." Rasahiko handed the men stripped red, white and blue arm bands. The government decided, and Barish International agreed that all American personnel should wear the same I.D. bands while exploring the moon. It is hoped that other governments will make the same ruling instead of allowing individual companies to each have their own I.D. It will simplify security when there are different government colonies here."

Mulvaina and Carver slipped the bands on.

"And now your helmets," said Rasahiko as he reached for one suspended from a cable hanging from a rafter. He rotated it.

The first thing that stood out to Mulvaina was a miniature t.v. screen mounted on the top-side of the helmet.

Rasahiko explained, "Detailed instructions for performing jobs are instantly available at the touch of a button. Also station instructions can be relayed."

Rasahiko pointed to a black bar on the left bottom side of the helmet. "Food bar," he stated. "This is sugar water." Next he turned the helmet over and pointed to its insides. A skull cap lining the helmet glistened with small silver caps. "Microphone pick-ups," he said. He looked at his watch then added, "I hope you'll be able to dress yourself alright next time but if you get confused or need some help, all you need to do is ring that buzzer at the side of the entrance door and assistance is on its way. Now it's time to get you to the transport tram which is waiting on the other side of a tunnel that lies beyond the door at the back of the room. Before you are about to exit the tunnel, there's a pull-out rest stop where you can put your helmet on. Once you place your helmet on, rotate it counterclockwise. It will automatically lock into position." Rasahiko's voice picked up speed, "Here's Julie to take you through the tunnel to the tram."

Mulvaina swung around. A helmetless extra-vehicular mobility unit stood facing them. Mulvaina thought Julie's head looked peculiarly small, as if it might be floating on top of an overinflated balloon. But her eyes he believed, were not only as beautiful as ever, but sparked with run-away excitement. Or was that just his hopeful imagination's interpretation. Just then Julie simply smiled in silent greeting. Mulvaina felt a sudden surge of warmth. A warmth that indeed defied the mechanical genius of his new water-cooled underwear and made his body boil with desire.

At the pullout, they all put on their helmets and rotated them counterclockwise. Just as their helmets locked, the tram arrived. Outside the tunnel a historical marker gleamed in the sun. The engraving read, "Here men from the planet Earth first set foot upon the moon, July 20, 1969, A.D. We came in peace for all mankind."

Mulvaina felt pride. Yes, it had been quite an achievement. He looked across the terrain as far as his eyes could behold. Such a tortured landscape. Mile after mile pock-marked with craters and strewn rocks of all shapes and sizes. Not exactly where he would personally want to build a country home for retirement. The person in the front seat of the tram turned around and nodded. Mulvaina knew it was Farnsworth who was taking them out to see the sights. In a few seconds, the tram lurched forward and then picked up speed racing off leaving moon dust behind.

After a few minutes Farnsworth broke the silence. "A few things are certain in life, everyone dies. A whore will always be a whore. And the unexpected is always expected in exploration."

Through the helmet speakers Mulvaina heard him loud and clear. Farnsworth's trinity of certainties stabbed at Mulvaina's sensibilities. There was something that he disliked about the man. Something that made him want to lay low like a dog who growls under his breath when he senses danger but doesn't see its face yet. Mulvaina looked at Farnsworth but it did no good. It was hard to judge a man that wore a space helmet over his face. Mulvaina looked out the window. He figured they were about four miles out from the main Lunar Base Camp complex.

The flat area of the moon where they had landed and where the base was established was now beginning to change. Mulvaina could see a few rounded low hills ahead on the horizon. In a matter of minutes the tram ran over the hill tops and rolled to a stop at the toe of their other side.

"Quarry Stop," came a voice over a penetrating tram speaker.

Even though his space helmet was equipped with a strongly tinted visor, Mulvaina squinted tightly as he came jumping off the tram. The sun set at a high angle overhead and sizzled everything it beamed on.

Less than one thousand feet in front of him was a large mining excavation area. Huge dinosaur-like machines dug their teeth into the face of the moon, lifted their heads, and spit out the contents within their jaws into large yellow dump trucks. Wickedly, lunar dust was everywhere.

Off to the right of the excavation area stood a field camp office, a crusher and a separator assembly. Farnsworth nodded towards Julie and she turned and stepped back inside the waiting tram. Then, Farnsworth motioned Mulvaina to follow and he led him over to the excavation site. "This area was just exposed about four hours ago," he explained. "We plan to extract some aggregate as well as mine some materials used in the lunarcrete."

Mulvaina noticed two of the workers were using surveying equipment and radiation detectors. "Why are they using radiation detectors?" he asked.

"The lunar surface," replied Farnsworth, "has been exposed to the solar wind for eons. That constant bombardment has left a sort of radioactive signature on the various minerals located here. We can get a fairly good idea of what is located beneath us by the spectrum of radioactive emission at any particular location." Farnsworth paused as if inhaling some extra oxygen. "Actually," he continued, "out in deep space, radiation, well, it comes from all directions. You might think the solid body of the Moon might block some radiation but not so. What happens is that when galactic cosmic rays collide with particles in the lunar surface, well they actually trigger little nuclear reactions that release yet more radiation in the form of neutrons. The lunar surface itself is radioactive. There's hot spots and cool spots. NASA back in the late 1990's used a Lunar Prospector probe to map neutron radiation of the moon to help design radiation shielding for our present day spacesuits and lunar habitat, moon vehicles and other equipment."

One of the workers interrupted Farnsworth by motioning him to come over to where they were working.

"Excuse me for a few moments," Farnsworth said, then in a bouncy motion walked over to the workers.

Mulvaina at once noticed the dusty moon surface took impressions of Farnsworth's boot prints very much like damp sand. He watched as the men talked for a few brief seconds then Mulvaina saw a worker hand Farnsworth a map. Mulvaina could see Farnsworth writing some kind of notation on the map. Probably naming the new site, Mulvaina thought.

One of the men turned and went over to a nearby land rover. What was he picking up? Mulvaina squinted. He couldn't tell until at last, the man was back with the group. It was a black carrying bag. The man stood there for a few seconds then he unzipped the bag and took out a camera. Mulvaina noticed some kind of paper was caught against his space glove and when he shifted the camera to his other hand, the paper whirl winded with the lunar dust. Then the man began taking photographs of the excavation area. Farnsworth was pointing in different angular directions and the photographer was taking his orders. Mulvaina observed Farnsworth was purposely stepping away from the shots so he would not be included in a photograph. Why, Mulvaina wondered, was Farnsworth so deliberately staying out of the photographs?

Mulvaina shifted ground. Would Farnsworth wave him over? Should he just wander over? He determined it was best to hold his position. His thoughts were interrupted by the photographer suddenly turning and walking back to the land rover. It was a distraction that almost worked except from the corner of his eye, Mulvaina saw Farnsworth bend down and sift some of the moon dirt through his space glove and then bring his fist straight up in a spontaneous gesture that seemed to indicate triumph.

Now a worker walked over to a nearby utility vehicle. He removed a large container marked "radiation shielding" and brought it back to the excavation site. He scooped up moon dirt and put it into the container and screwed the lid on tightly. Another man carried it over to a truck and loaded it aboard.

At last, as if remembering there was a bystander waiting, Farnsworth looked up in Mulvaina's direction and began hastily bouncing back towards him.

When they were within speaking range Mulvaina commented, "That's a pretty heavily shielded container."

Caught by surprise by the remark, Farnsworth stammered out, "Yes. Why, yes. It is." Then he added in a more controlled tone, "We need to take precautions with this lunar material. It can be dangerous if not handled properly."

Mulvaina followed Farnsworth's boot-prints to the field office. "Mulvaina," said Farnsworth, "just leave your space helmet on, we're only going to be inside for a few minutes."

Inside Mulvaina could see there were several computers analyzing the readout from the radiation detectors and the surveying equipment. Hanging on the walls were photographs of excavation sites. "Nice photography work," remarked Mulvaina. "Is this work done by the same photographer whose work is displayed on the walls of the living quarters of the moon base?"

"Yes," answered Farnsworth without further input.

Farnsworth moved towards a plotting machine. Mulvaina followed him. "All the data we collect during our surveys is fed into the computer. It plots the location of each of our survey points as well as noting the minerals suspected to lie below the surface, based upon the analysis of the detector's spectral data."

"Looks complicated. How do you keep track of all this?" Mulvaina asked.

"It's tricky. We have over six hundred maps covering nearly thirty square miles of the lunar surface around the base and that is just a fraction of the total job we have left to do."

"Have you ever found anything of interest other than what you need for lunarcrete?" inquired Mulvaina.

"No, nothing significant," Farnsworth replied quickly. Then shifting his weight he added, "Maybe a few trace elements here and there, a meteorite or two, but on the whole the lunar surface is I would say homogenous with basalt and silicates and the like."

Mulvaina noted the rote tone of Farnsworth's speech and the fact that one of the workers in the office had quietly and quickly rolled up all the surveying maps laying on the desk tops.

CHAPTER 16

"I really don't like you doing this, Robin. Can't I talk you out of it?" pleaded Joe Grimaldi.

"Just give me a hand getting suited up and a handshake for luck. That's all you have to do," answered Mulvaina strongly with no lack of determination in his voice.

"Shit," replied Grimaldi as he lifted one of the space suits off from the hanging bars. Then he added, "It's not all I have to do. I won't let you go alone. I have us both cleared on the computer to go out sightseeing to the radio astronomical observatory. It is quite a distance from the base and a remote site usually not manned. We should have plenty of time to have you over to the excavation site and back. I got access to a land rover so that eliminates the tram driver but I've got to be your driver. What the hell, I know where to go. Can't take a chance you'll get lost and dead."

"I'm glad I have a trusted friend up here. Things are getting somewhat complicated. There is more than meets the initial investigative eye here, old buddy," Mulvaina replied.

Soon the two men were completely suited and heading down the tunnel and over to the land rover parking station.

"This is much more fun than the tram," said Grimaldi as they jumped in. "Fasten your seat old man and hold on for an "E-Ticket" ride!" Mulvaina chuckled under his breath at Grimaldi's reference to a long ago ticket for the most exciting attractions at a popular amusement park in the mid-twentieth century.

Out in the open, bouncing around in the rover, for the first time since he stepped foot on the moon, Mulvaina felt relaxed and not on the defensive. He inhaled deeply the oxygen. Like any tourist in a strange place he took in the scenery.

Grimaldi drove away from the base until he was sure they were totally out of sight and once the land rover was behind a small rise he steered the vehicle off the main tract. He accelerated the rover to 15 m.p.h. and Mulvaina could feel the bounce gaining strength now and had to admit it was quite comparable to a thrilling carnival ride he remembered going on as a young boy. In a few minutes, Mulvaina could see that they were coming up behind the quarry.

Grimaldi slowed the rover and eased in behind the quarry like a cat creeping up towards a bird. Satisfied with the hidden position of the rover, Grimaldi turned off the motor. In the distance all was empty. The workers were obviously all back at the moon base. The equipment lay shut down like prehistoric monsters in a diorama.

Mulvaina began to step out of the rover, but suddenly realized dismounting the vehicle with a spacesuit took a bit of doing. He finally turned sideways, then stepped off in sort of a jumping jack motion. It worked.

Grimaldi reached under the seat of the rover and hit a release button, and pulled out stainless steel tongs and a small stainless scoop tool, both attached with long, narrow extension handles.

"Use the scoop to pick up small rocks," Grimaldi said. Then he added in a straight forward instructive tone, "use the mouse trap-like devise to collect your soil sample. Open and press down on to the surface. This cloth patch on the tool's face will collect the upper most particles of lunar material from the surface. When you lift the tool up, it will spring shut and protect your sample." Grimaldi paused and looked straight through Mulvaina's space helmet and caught his eyes, "be quick. All looks calm, but you never can tell what might bring someone out this way."

Mulvaina went cautiously down the small hill and peered into the field office window. All lights were out. He proceeded to the area where he judged Farnsworth had stood with the workmen and taken a sample of moon soil. There were so many tracks crisscrossing in the sand from the wheels of the machinery that Mulvaina thought he would never be able to determine the particular spot, and he was just about to take a random sample when to his right, about twenty feet, he spotted something glistening. He walked over to it. It was a small flat piece of an antistatic material. He thought for a moment. Of course, photographers sometimes wrapped their memory sticks in metallic sheen bags when storing them for long periods of time. Mulvaina spontaneously reached for it, but he found the stiffness of his space suite made it difficult to bend over. He sort of laughed at himself, and then Mulvaina maneuvered his mouse trap-like tool and pressed down into the moon soil. Yes, he thought, this had been the spot from which Farnsworth had taken his sample. As he pulled his tool up, it sprang shut protecting his sample.

Suddenly from faraway headlights began approaching. Mulvaina saw the lights and tucked the tools against his side, and with giant strides made his way over to hide behind one of the large quarry pieces of equipment.

A lunar rover came bouncing forward and stopped right in front of the field office. Someone, unrecognizable in their spacesuit, jumped off and went inside the field office. After a few minutes he came out and headed for the machinery.

Shit, now what am I going to do? thought Mulvaina. But before he could formulate any plan of action, the someone in the spacesuit was climbing aboard the very machine Mulvaina was hiding behind and already starting the engine. Mulvaina prayed he wouldn't go in reverse. The machine lurched forward and headed towards the field office. Mulvaina crept as best as he could behind the machine thankful at least that the space helmet kept out all the lunar dust that cloaked him. As soon as Mulvaina felt he was close enough to make a dash across the rise and back to Gramaldi, he put all his energy into full stride and did what later he described to Gramaldi as a bounce for his life.

CHAPTER 17

A voice came over the intercom. "Please approach the boarding gate if you are returning to Earth on today's space shuttle."

Mulvaina directed his attention to Julie. Her eyes had lost their sparkle and, although incredibly beautiful, were also sad. Or did he flatter himself Mulvaina wondered. Perhaps he just wanted her to be sad at his leaving. Perhaps her eyes only showed fatigue. He denied that. He felt a tugging at his heart. He had to admit these past few days with her had left him now with a gnawing feeling and a regret at leaving.

As if to answer his thoughts Julie asked softly, "We'll be seeing each other again soon won't we?" Then as if to insure a positive answer she handed him some papers, "The reports you asked for. If you have any questions about them once you get back to Earth, please call me."

"Thanks," said Mulvaina. "I may need to return soon for further investigation. Who knows," he paused for just a moment. There was so much more he wanted to say but opportunity was limited with so many people standing near. He wanted to kiss Julie good-bye, but somehow it seemed inappropriate under the circumstances. Finally he asked, "Do you have any reason to be coming back to Earth?"

Julie simply nodded her head in answer.

Mulvaina understood and knew that time would bring them together again. He turned towards John Farnsworth. "Your operation here has fascinated me."

"Glad to see someone taking an interest in it. Have a safe trip home," Farnsworth said with what Mulvaina felt was too much insincere enthusiasm.

Mulvaina turned and offered a handshake to Fred Jones. "Thanks, Fred, for giving me the run of the base. It made my job much easier."

"Well, I'm the one that would like to thank you. At, may I say, at the very risk of your own life, you uncovered that Rotacello fellow and that has helped everyone of us up here. In fact, I have a little something for you to show our gratitude for your work." Jones reached into a brown plastic bag and took out a red, white, and blue stripped wrapped gift box and handed it to Mulvaina.

"Why thank you," said Mulvaina as he took the gift. Then rather shyly added, "I love surprises."

Everyone laughed with good humor.

"Please, open it now," said Julie. "You have time. The space shuttle attendant knows you are boarding. This isn't LAX. They'll wait for you."

"O.K.," said Mulvaina gladly. He neatly unwrapped the package and opened the box. "Wow! What a great memento," Mulvaina said with genuine meaning. He held up a large key.

"It's cast in lunarcrete," said Jones.

"How appropriate," said Mulvaina and then he read the inscribed words:

Lunar Base Camp, Barish International.

Everyone clapped. Mulvaina felt his cheeks turn red with warmth from a school-boy-like embarrassment.

"I had one of our carpenters make the form," said Jones, "and John contributed the lunarcrete."

"That's good stuff. Should test at least at 3500 psi, provided Fred installed it right," said Farnsworth.

"I took special care to install it right, just like I do with all the lunarcrete here," said Jones with what Mulvaina considered a serious tone of voice.

"Well then, Mr. Mulvaina, maybe you had better give that key a little extra special handling," said Farnsworth.

Mulvaina noted the sarcasm. What rivalry or problem

existed between Jones and Farnsworth, he wondered. He wished he had a little more time to explore it.

"I expect you to keep your lunar memento forever Robin, for it will indeed open the doors of this lunar base for you," said Jones as he thrust his hand out quickly and gave Mulvaina a very firm handshake.

It seemed to Mulvaina that Jones was being a little overemotional but, perhaps that was the nature of the man. At any rate all the fanfare was beginning to upset him and was making leaving Julie even more regretful. "I appreciate it. Thank you. You can be sure I will always treasure it," Mulvaina said. Then he thought what the hell, emotion seems to be quite accepted in this scenario of departure, and so he quickly stepped towards Julie and kissed her with such passion that it surprised himself.

Then without another word, Mulvaina turned and walked down the corridor to board the shuttle waiting to return home to Earth.

CHAPTER 18

Mulvaina and Thomas Helms sat alone in their office of M.F.P. Associates. Coffee stained paper cups and an empty bagel box was evidence that they had worked right through the night and into the new morning. Mulvaina turned another page of the report he was reading. Helms closed the report he was reading, shifted in his chair, then stretched up taller in his seat. He took a deep breath then said, "The pattern appears conclusive."

"What's that, Thomas?" Mulvaina asked.

"I would guess that in the past twelve months Soots and Jones have been selling materials meant for the lunar base to other people on Earth, and falsifying records and expense accounts. They have also embezzled Barish International for at least a million dollars," Helms stated loudly and clearly.

"Let me see those figures," said Mulvaina.

Helms brought his ledger sheets over to Mulvaina's desk. "Here's the majority of funds lost in fraudulent claims of lost or damaged shipments handled by one of the companies owned by Harry Sellers."

"Very interesting," said Mulvaina as he surveyed the figures. "I need to get in touch with Jeff Zallos, the owner of that all-terrain vehicle business, and have a talk with him."

"How are you going to present this embezzlement information to Mr. Barish?" asked Helms.

"I'm not sure yet. When is the next shuttle due to arrive back here from the moon?" Mulvaina asked while looking at his watch.

"About five-thirty a.m. tomorrow morning," replied Helms. Then he asked, "What are you thinking?"

"From this report on Lunarcrete, you indicate the company

owns some additional land just east of their main desert facility."

"That's right," answered Helms, "about thirty miles east of it. Their records show the land is undeveloped and in a rather desolate area."

"Are you free tomorrow morning?" asked Mulvaina.

"Alright," Helms replied knowing Mulvaina had really implied a directive not a question.

Mulvaina grabbed his cell lying on the desk and dialed a long distant number. After a few seconds, he enthusiastically said, "How's the all-terrain vehicle business doing, Jeff? Great!" Then in a most persuasive tone Mulvaina added, "Say, Jeff, I wonder if I might just ask a special favor of you?"

....

The yuccas stood like watchful sentinels in the pre-dawn darkness waiting in anticipation of the advancement of the vehicle that camouflaged itself on the small hilltop.

Mulvaina peered across the dark desert through his field binoculars. "How much longer before the shuttle?" he whispered as if the yuccas had a thousand spying ears.

Helms looked down at his watch and concentrated hard on the position of its hands. "I would say about two minutes."

They sat in silence anticipating the accuracy of their reasoning and figuring.

"Look. Here. It's coming," whispered Mulvaina.

Helms peered hard into the sky, and soon off to the west he, too, saw the unmistakable gleaming, fiery trail of the re-entering shuttle. Then, like parachuting fireflies, a cluster of small freight pods re-entered.

"Keep your eyes on the freight pods, Thomas," said Mulvaina with urgency.

Mulvaina watched as the shuttle glided silently overhead at high altitude, preparing to bank for its final turn and alignment with the space pad nearly fifty miles away.

"I only count six chutes. I guess they've lost a couple this time," said Helms.

"No, they haven't. They are all accounted for," said Mulvaina with certainty.

"I thought there were suppose to be eight pods on board," said Helms somewhat confused.

"That's right," answered Mulvaina.

"Do you see the other two? I don't," said Helms.

"There," said Mulvaina and he pointed directly east.

Helms looked through his binoculars. To the east, about five miles from them, two freight pods were floating to the desert floor. "I'll be dammed!" uttered Helms. Then he added, "Should we pursue?"

"Hell, yes," answered Mulvaina.

Helms lifted off the camouflage and started up the exotic open-top all-terrain vehicle and accelerated forward. "Reminds me of the moon," said Mulvaina and for a few seconds he let himself be warmed by pleasant, happy memories of Julie.

Helms stopped the vehicle just below the top of a sand dune. Cautiously Mulvaina and Helms got out and ran to the top of the hill and laid belly down. They could clearly see the two errant pods lying conspicuously on the desert floor. They hadn't laid there long when the silence was broken by the disruptive sound of distant motors. Shortly, two desert trucks came wheeling their way across the sand and pulled up along the side of the pods. A man, dressed in white coveralls, got out. Mulvania could see that the man carried a radiation detector over to the pods. The man spent a few minutes inspecting the pods and then he waved his arm in a definite gesture signifying a signal to someone. Soon, another man, also dressed in white coveralls, got out of the truck. The men talked for a few moments and then walked over to the pods. The man with the radiation detector waved it over the pods. Then, seemingly satisfied the two men lifted each pod onto the truck. Finished, they drove off and disappeared into the rising sun.

When Mulvaina thought a safe amount of time had put

distance between them, he told Helms to follow the tread tracks of the men's vehicle. The sun was almost mid-way into the sky now and the desert was waking and smelled fresh and looked deceivingly inviting. After about twenty minutes or so the tread marks deadened onto what looked like a well traveled dirt road.

"It's getting interesting," said Helms.

"I love the reward of adventure this job affords," said Mulvaina not so much with sarcasm as true enthusiasm.

The dirt road lead into a narrow canyon and the air was dusty and although irritating to Mulvaina's throat it told him he was definitely following the trail of trucks ahead. Suddenly, they came to a point where a large ravine crossed the path. "We're in for one hell of a bumpy ride," said Helms.

"Hold on and watch this," said Mulvaina with a chuckle. He leaned over and reached under Helms and pushed a black button under the steering wheel. There was a sudden jolting motion and then the exotic all-terrain vehicle was airborne, hovering a few feet off the ground and surmounting the rocky obstacles on the terrain with the greatest of ease.

It seemed only seconds later that Mulvaina found himself quickly putting the vehicle into reverse, skimming back a hundred feet, and pressing another button so that with somewhat of a jolt, not unlike a quick break stop, the vehicle came to a dead stop on flat ground. "God, I hope no one observed us. That was a close call," said Mulvaina.

"It looked like a damn compound of some sorts those trucks drove into," added Helms.

"I was concentrating on pressing the correct button on this panel. I didn't catch too much detail. Did you?" asked Mulvaina.

"Yes, I think so," answered Helms. "Electrified fence. Several guard towers. A clear area. Several large buildings. I got an overall impression that there were a lot of trucks parked around the buildings."

"Sort of like covered wagons around a campfire," said Mulvaina.

"Interesting history correlation, but yes, I guess in that

same manner," answered Helms.

"Anything else?" asked Mulvaina.

"Lots of white coveralls walking around. That's all I took in."

"You did damn good for just a few seconds. Yes, you sure did, Helms," said Mulvaina.

"I graduated in the top five of my training class," Helms answered proudly.

"I know. That is exactly why I hired you," Mulvaina replied.

"Still, I feel I have a lot to learn about this business and I intend to learn it from you. They say you're the best. So what do we do now, Robin?"

"Wait," replied Mulvaina. "Just wait and watch until it feels right."

The sun rose higher and higher into the sky. The sunlight reflecting from the almost bare earth was becoming blinding. Mulvaina kept lowering his binoculars and wiping the perspiration from his face. Helms did the same. The men watched and waited in silence. Once Mulvaina got up and walked over to the vehicle and brought back two canteens of water. He handed one to Helms but didn't say a word. It would have been, he felt, an unnecessary effort. About noon a wind came up. At first it was a welcomed relief, but not for long as it gathered up a somewhat demonic force and cursed the two men with a fine dust that filled their eyes, noses, and throats.

Suddenly, a loud screeching sound filled the sky and both Mulvaina and Helms rolled to their backs instantly and let out an instinctual growl from the depths of their being as they saw circling overhead, slow and heavy, a large ominous looking buzzard.

The wind picked up more speed and thickened the dusty air. Mulvaina began to cough in a chocking like manner. He sat up trying to clear his lungs and as he did so, he saw a cloud of dust moving forward in their direction. Mulvaina grabbed Helms by the forearm and pulled him into a sitting up position. Then he pointed towards the cloud, quickly relayed a plan of action, and then jumped to his feet and ran off in the direction of the coming cloud.

The approaching flatbed truck came slowing down to round a curve. The driver was thumping his hand against the steering wheel keeping beat to the music that poured into his head from his earphones. As the truck came out of the curve, Mulvaina jumped aboard and quickly hid amongst the crates loaded on the truck.

Soon the truck approached the main gate of the compound. Mulvaina maneuvered up closer to the cab of the truck where the crates were packed more densely. He heard the guard say, "Good morning, Ray. How was the drive?"

Ray answered huskily, "F...ing hot coming over here. I need a cold beer."

The guard laughed robustly. "Have one for me too, buddy. I think it's shit that they don't let us have any cold beer out here at the gate house. A shit guard," the guard stressed his title then added, "who's guarding what? Who is ever going to find their way out to this hell-hole of a place unless they're told to come out here, anyway?"

"Yea, I agree, replied Ray. "Whoever's running this place is an absolute paranoid asshole. Shit, it's so damn hot out here! I'll sneak you a cold beer after I've downed a few."

"Don't forget, Ray, bring me back a beer or two," hollered the guard as the truck rolled into the compound.

The driver promptly drove over to a loading door on a south facing portion of the nearest building. He maneuvered the truck around so that its rear was backed into the unloading zone. He got out, walked behind the truck and opened the tailgate, and slid the first crate to the edge. He looked up and around. "Shit! Where in the hell are you lazy son of bitches," he called out. Not seeing anyone responding, he trudged over to the other side of the building and entered a door marked simply "O".

As the driver disappeared inside, Mulvaina peered out from behind the crates, appraised the situation for himself and said under his breath, "Thank you," then jumped down off the truck and walked purposely through the loading door and into the building. Inside his eyes were blinded by the darkness. He groped his way to some boxes and crouched behind them and waited for his eyes to adjust. A fuzzy sign came finally into focus. Mulvaina made out the words: Locker Room. He surveyed the rest of the inside area and felt assured that he was alone. He looked for surveillance cameras and saw none. He maneuvered across the room shielding himself behind the height of the boxes.

He entered the locker room cautiously, his hand positioned for a quick draw of his revolver. He was relieved to find the room was totally empty. A long narrow bench stood between two rows of lockers and Mulvaina felt like Lady Luck was with him when he saw several white coveralls sprawled over a bench.

Mulvaina hastily shuffled through the overalls holding up one longer looking pair against his body for a moment, then quickly changed. Just as he zipped up the fly, Mulvaina heard the sound of voices approaching. He reacted instantly. The locker room door swung open, and two heavy set men, one with a scraggly brown beard and a broad forehead, and another with thick black-rimmed glasses and short cut sandy hair, walked in.

Mulvaina could hear a locker open and a faucet running. He tried to curl up his toes and force back his shoes, but to no avail. He wondered if the men would notice the toes of his shoes sticking out from behind the water closet door that he had found seconds before they came closer. He held his revolver close to his chest and waited with his eyes closed, concentrating hard so that he heard even the slightest sound the men made.

"I'm so f...ing sick of this desert," one of the men blurted out as he slammed a locker door.

"Watch it," said the other calmly.

"I think doing time beats this rap," the man continued.

"You owe Salvo," the other man insisted.

"I don't owe anyone. Anyone. Got that," the agitated man's voice became more angry.

"Sure," said the other man calmly.

A locker door slammed shut and then Mulvaina could tell

the voices were drifting across the room and he sighed with relief. Mulvaina came out of hiding and slipped out of the locker room, the white overalls giving him a sense of disguised confidence. He walked nonchalantly around the structure and entered the main building. Inside was a transit shed full of crate boxes loaded on pallets. A low humming from an air conditioning unit filled the space, but besides that Mulvaina quickly surmised that the shed was silent and without human movement. He walked around the sides of boxes noting the shipping labels and memorizing them. Southwest Nuclear Fuels – Denver, Colorado. Oregon Gas and Electrical Company, Nuclear Division. New Mexico Edison, Cache Creek Thermonuclear Power Station. Pieces in the puzzle were beginning to fit. Mulvaina hid behind some of the boxes and decided to wait. After all, he thought, life wasn't worth living without taking chances and this could just be the connection that brought the whole case together. If he hit it big, it was even possible Barish would give him a bonus and that just might put him into such an economic position that he might be able to consider getting to know Julie a whole lot better. The thought gave him courage as he heard a truck approaching.

The driver left the motor running. Obviously, he intended to stop only for a few minutes, Mulvaina thought. The man walked into the shed. Mulvaina waited a moment longer, then he stepped forward carrying a smaller box with him. He intended to carry it to the truck and hop on board and see where it was going and what it was, but just as he rounded a stack of high boxes he collided with two men. Mulvaina kept his head low and didn't look up. Were these the two men he saw earlier in the locker?

"Stupid ass. Watch where you are going," yelled one of the men.

Mulvaina recognized the voice. Holy shit, he thought, it's Salvo. Mulvaina swung his fist into the belly of the other man and took off running.

"Stop, him. Stop that stupid ass," screamed the same voice and Mulvaina knew without a doubt it was Salvo.

Mulvaina spurted to the waiting truck, jumped in, was

thankful it was an old late model, and gunned it into reverse. When he was in the middle of the clearing he swung it around and accelerated towards the main gate. Like a knight of old he charged at the guardsman with the confidence of right and justice on his side. The guard perceiving death, threw himself out of the way just seconds before Mulvaina crashed the truck through the gate.

....

Mulvaina pushed the already heavily vibrating truck to 80 m.p.h. and sped out of the canyon and towards the desert. Just as he was pulling out of the canyon curve, Mulvaina saw a most welcome sight. Helms, like a devoted squire, was idling the all-terrain vehicle. And, even in the tenseness of the moment, Mulvaina could, if not see, at least feel, a wide boyish grin on Helm's face. Mulvaina skidded to a stop and ran over to the ATV.

Helms pushed the green button under the steering wheel and the ATV sprouted a pair of wings and the men soared a hundred feet above the desert floor and flew off at a hundred miles per hour. Mulvaina turned towards Helms but before he could say anything, Helms said, "I've been glancing at the control manual off and on while you were in the building."

"Ummm," sighed Mulvaina. "Good for me, you weren't glancing off when I made my Olympic dash to the truck!"

"Never fear, Helms is here," Helms said light heartily.

"My life will depend on it," Mulvaina answered back seriously.

"Well, the coast is clear now," he retorted and reached back with his right hand and lifted the cover of the ice chest and pulled out a bottle of water and handed it to Mulvaina. "Flying this baby is a dream," he said relaxing and enjoying what he was doing.

"Don't get too happy. I ran into Salvo inside that shed. That asshole is no dummy. He's not just going to let us fly away into the sunset and live happily ever after." He passed his drink to

Helms.

Helms took a gulp and leaned back in the seat. Mulvaina suddenly straighten up in his. "Do you hear that?" he asked.

"My stomach just growled," answered Helms.

"No, not that. Blades against the wind," said Mulvaina.

"Just your imagination," Helms replied.

"No. It's coming. I know it in my bones." Mulvaina grabbed up his binoculars and looked to the rear. His instintive feeling was confirmed. A flickering gleam way off in the fathomless distance caught his eye. Mulvaina felt uneasy. He knew Salvo was coming for revenge. The flickering gleam was advancing and gaining on them. Mulvaina felt his heart pumping quicker, "Will this ATV go any faster?" he asked nervously.

"It's full speed. Do you see something?" asked Helms.

"Look in your rear view mirror right now," said Mulvaina in a command tone.

Helms looked. Mulvaina put down his binoculars. They were unnecessary. The flickering gleam was nearer and nearer and becoming bigger and more distinct. Helms bit down on his lip with anxiety. Mulvaina muttered, "This doubtlessly will be a perilous adventure."

Both Mulvaina and Helms simultaneously saw the flickering gleam turn to whirl-winding metal blades as a huge white helicopter began to swoop down towards them.

Mulvaina's courage quivered as he recognized the helicopter model. "It's a cobra three, Helms. Among other things, it's armed with a laser cannon."

Mulvaina reached down and opened a door to a small compartment area labeled Defense Panel. He flipped a switch labeled Laser Defense. At the rear of the ATV two sensors rose up and pointed in the direction of the chopper.

"Here it comes," said Mulvaina. "Hold the hell on tight."

The chopper's engine exhaust turned to an eerie glow. Instantly, the ATV's sensors released a thick cloud of white smoke-like substance that enveloped the rear body of the ATV. A second later a beam shot forward from the chopper and collided against the thick cloud. There was a flash of light like a bolt of lightning and a deafening clap like thunder. The ATV shook violently and then after a few seconds stabilized.

"God! How long can we keep this up?" exclaimed Helms.

"Zallos only installed four canisters of gas. It takes two minutes before they can fire their cannon again," answered Mulvaina rather matter-of-fact.

Mulvaina turned around and pushed aside the ice chest. He grabbed a handle and pulled up hard and a shallow compartment holding an automatic rifle came into view. Mulvaina grabbed the rifle up and laid it across his lap. "Do you still know how to use one of these, Helms?" he asked.

Before Helms could answer, suddenly about two hundred yards away, a fat, whopping metal satan of revenge appeared parallel to the ATV. The chopper was so close Mulvaina thrust the rifle at Helms and grabbed the steering wheel. Amidst the frenzy of fire spewing from the rifle, Mulvaina banked the ATV sharply away from the chopper.

The chopper pulled up and banked away, made a wide circle, and then lined up a distance behind the ATV.

"Hold on. Here we go again," said Mulvaina.

Once again the chopper's engine exhaust became an eerie glow. The ATV sensors triggered another canister of gas and the thick white cloud enveloped its rear. There was a flash of light and a clap of thunder that roared clear across the desert floor. The ATV shook more violently than the last time but at last stabilized.

Mulvaina guided the ATV between two ridges of a desert mountain range. The chopper edged alongside the ATV at a short distance. Soon bullets danced off the rocks from the top of the ridge and the range echoed a warring song.

Mulvaina could see up ahead a narrow ravine. He banked the ATV away from the chopper and headed down the ravine. The chopper pursued with fiery insistence and was quickly catching up. Again the chopper's engine became an eerie glow and again the ATV's sensors triggered the canisters of gas and the thick white cloud enveloped its rear. Mulvaina tightened his grip on the steering wheel.

Just as the chopper fired its laser cannon, there was a sudden momentary updraft and the laser beam veered slightly, but still enough so that it missed the ATV and struck the side of the ravine. There was a violent explosion. Sparks and rubble scattered throughout the sky.

Mulvaina guided the ATV down to the base of the mountain and began following a rough road cut through its bottom. The chopper followed, zig-zagging along the course of the road, firing off a multitude of automatic shots. Mulvaina with steadfast grip on the steering wheel rocked the ATV up and down in a rhythmic pattern that was successfully evading the gun fire.

Suddenly Mulvaina spotted a low saddle in the mountain ridge. He turned into it quickly. Too soon again the chopper came like a metallic bat from hell and was lining up behind them.

The chopper's engine turned an eerie glow, the ATV enveloped itself in the white cloud. Mulvaina pulled up on the steering wheel with all his strength and the ATV reared like a gallant war horse and the laser beam whizzed through the sky and struck the ground below mercilessly. Mulvaina continued to let the ATV climb until it was over the saddle and into a canyon beyond.

Within minutes the chopper was right behind them again. The chopper's engine turned its eerie glow. The ATV's sensors reacted. The beam collided. The bolt of lightning seared the thick white cloud. A thunderclap rolled throughout the canyon. The ATV shook more violently and much longer than the last time but, at last, it finally did stabilize.

"Come on fire. Fire," screamed Mulvaina at the top of his voice as if the mere volume of it would carry it across the sky to the chopper's occupants' ears.

"Have you gone crazy! I don't want to die yet," exclaimed Helms.

Once again the chopper's engine became an eerie glow. The ATV sensors tried to react but the canisters were all used up. There was no forthcoming thick white cloud.

"God have mercy on us," uttered Helms.

Suddenly, the chopper's engine flashed of fire. Instantly, two ejection seats came bursting into view. Mulvaina counted out the seconds. One. Two. With fury the chopper exploded into a million metal fragments.

"They didn't wait long enough between laser beam discharges," Mulvaina said simply.

Mulvaina circled the ATV back to the area where the men had ejected. He looked down. One man was standing and untying yellow parachute cords. Another man laid sprawled across a mammoth rock, his lips puckered and contorted with pain, but Mulvaina could see that it was the face of Salvo.

Mulvaina turned the ATV west to head home. It was after all, war; perhaps of an individual kind, and one dressed in revenge, but none the less, it was war. Mulvaina pressed down on the accelerator and left the two men to now fight battle against the cruel sun.

CHAPTER 19

"I understand the sensitivity with which you asked me to handle this matter, Mr. Mulvaina, and you can be assured that I will. But, I must tell you that what I have discovered about this ore sample you brought me is something which requires and I stress requires the utmost caution and discretion," said Dr. James Schmidt. He leafed through a pile of computer print-outs in front of him as somewhat of a symbolic gesture.

"I understand requirements well," said Mulvaina. "What is it that I've brought you exactly?"

Dr. Schmidt shifted his position and straighten the upper frames of his smokey-colored glasses. "Ever heard of Ivy Mike?"

"Yes," said Mulvaina, "that was the code name for the United States first nuclear device."

"The first hydrogen bomb successfully detonated on November 1, 1952 by our Air Force over the Pacific; actually on the island of Elugelab in Enewetak Atoll. Those early devices consisted of an atomic bomb which detonated and ignited a small quantity of cryogenic deuterium located inside of it," said Dr. Schmidt.

"What do you mean? Are we talking about frozen?" asked Mulvaina.

"No. Liquefied, not frozen. Such devices were capable of producing tremendous explosions. In fact, the Soviets detonated their first H-bomb in August 1953. They were able to do so only two years after us because there was a Soviet spy at Los Alamos, the U.S. research facility where the bomb was created. In fact, I think the Soviets detonated an H-Bomb which was rated I believe at over a hundred megatons. But while capable of tremendous displays, such devices were unpractical for use as weapons."

"Why was that?" asked Mulvaina trying in his mind to relate the pieces of what Dr. Schmidt was telling him and anticipate the conclusion.

"Because," explained Dr. Schmidt, "after a few hours the liquid would evaporate, and you no longer had a hydrogen bomb but instead a low yield atomic bomb."

Mulvaina began to understand. "A very unpractical weapon for standing months or even years on nuclear alert," he said.

"Yes, exactly," stated Dr. Schmidt. "Most people don't realize this "Mike" Device was essentially a building designed more like a factory then a weapon."

Helms spoke up. "So how did they overcome the problem?"

"Actually, they didn't. Modern nuclear arsenals conceal a serious vulnerability," answered Dr. Schmidt. He stroked his graying beard for a moment then continued, "All during the period of the first and second cold wars, the Atomic Energy Commission created a ruse whereby they had everyone convinced that the United States was building weapon devices which contained tritium by a technique known as hydrogenization."

"I've heard the term, but what is it?" asked Mulvaina.

"It's the tendency of certain materials, such as lithium, to absorb gaseous hydrogen and store it at great densities approaching that of liquid hydrogen."

"I get it. The host material acts like a sponge, holding the tritium and thus creating weapons which can be stored for longer periods of time," said Helms like an enlightened schoolboy.

"Or so it was in theory," said Dr. Schmidt. He bit his lip, hesitating for a moment, then continued, "But in practice it was found that there was a time discrepancy for getting the required densities. And that time, required to get proper density," he paused for a moment to add dramatic impact, "approached several hundred years." He raised his eyebrows waiting in anticipation for an excited response. Not getting an immediate one he added, "This was combined with the approximate half-life of tritium."

"Half-life," Helms interrupted.

Tritium, itself, only has a half-life of 12.5 days severely limiting the shelf life of bombs," answered Dr. Schmidt. Then he added, "A bigger problem is that tritium isn't found in nature. For a while researchers used lithium which got rid of the half-life problem but the particular isotope of lithium needed was prohibitively too expensive to manufacture, and a true tritium bomb seemed an impossible dream."

Astonished by what he was hearing, Mulvaina asked, "Do you mean all during the cold wars there were never any hydrogen bombs placed on nuclear missiles aimed at all moments at Russia and aimed at all moments at the U.S.?"

"Let's just say that in a hundred years or so, when this knowledge becomes public, people then will look upon the people of the late twentieth century much like we look upon those people of the dark ages who feared fire-breathing dragons."

"How?" asked Helms in disbelief.

"Simple," said Dr. Schmidt. "The United States convinced, brainwashed, the world that they had solid state nuclear weapons. Russia, not willing to admit her own technical inability, and believing the American ruse, acted as if she too had solid state nuclear weapons. And so it went for decades, each side knowing they had what the old Chinese Mao once called , "a paper tiger," but not sure if the other side was equally impotent."

"Let's get back to these moon samples. How do the samples relate?" inquired Mulvaina.

"What man was incapable of doing in the most sophisticated laboratories, nature has evidently done on the moon. The ore samples you brought back have been hydrogenised with tritium to an extent making them suitable for nuclear weapons." Dr. Schmidt took a breath as if to clear the air. Then he continued, "More importantly, in my opinion, these ore sample are suitable as fuel in thermo-nuclear reactors. The problems which currently plague the thermo-nuclear reactor industry is the inability to find suitable fuel in sufficient quantity. If there is much more of this material it would dramatically release the nuclear power industry of nearly all of its problems."

"Ah," sighed Helms and then added with insight, "and whoever had control of those ore deposits would soon become a very rich man."

"Incredibly rich and incredibly powerful," said Mulvaina. "I want to thank you doctor for all of your time and help in this matter."

"You're welcome," answered Dr. Schmidt. He held out his hand. "I hope your visit to our university's physics laboratory was informative today. I feel we have the best one in the United States. I'm sure if you want a second opinion you'll find my findings conclusive."

"There's really no need for that," said Mulvaina. "Your reputation doctor is undisputable and invaluable in helping in our investigation of this case we are working on."

CHAPTER 20

Mulvaina looked up from the pile of papers on his desk and gazed out the window. It was gray and misting. "Helms are we about ready to leave for the space port?"

"In about thirty minutes or less. I'm about finished now," replied Helms.

"Be sure to let me know once you have background information on South West Nuclear Fuels," said Mulvaina.

"Of course. Immediately."

"Good. And find out whatever you can about the status of Salvo and the pilot of his helicopter."

"As of an hour ago, Salvo was still unconscious."

"Good." Mulvaina stretched back in his chair and took a deep breath and then exhaled slowly. "So long as Salvo is unconscious, we're safe."

"Are you sure you'll be safe up on the moon? I don't trust their security worth a damn. If you ask me I think it has been manipulated," said Helms.

"Evil manipulation," Mulvaina answered silently. "Glad you care," Mulvaina said out loud and winked good naturedly at Helms. "I'll watch myself. It's necessary to get to the bottom of this. Something tells me that Fellows plays a key role in this, but just exactly how, I don't know." Mulvaina picked up the lunarcrete key that had been presented to him as he left the moon. "Pretty impressive paper weight, huh, Helms?"

"Clever gift idea for the Earth man that has everything!" said Helms in a mimicking chuckle.

Mulvaina sat the paperweight back down on his desk, ran his forefinger across it lightly several times, then said seriously, "Guard it with your life while I'm gone, Helms, it may be more than meets the eye.”

....

Mulvaina had hoped the next three travelling days up to the moon would give him the opportunity to sort the data running through his mind. But instead he found himself sitting next to an enthusiastic member of the Earth-Moon Explorers. Always believing there was something more than magic in why we have matched meetings with strangers, as in the case of who we sit next to during a flight, Mulvaina accepted his seat companion's four days of talkative interactions as part of synchronicity and that there was something for him to learn from the encounter that would be helpful either for the investigation or for his individual life; either as a necessity or as a message that would propel him towards his happiness goals.

It all started with his seat companion's extra-ordinary introduction, “Say, isn't this a great ride? By the way, my name is Atsa, means Eagle. Eagle medicine is the ability to live in the realm of the spirit and yet remain connected to the realm of the Earth. Eagle soars above the clouds and can observe the pattern of life on Earth. I guess it's my name that has giving me such passion to want to soar above the ordinary happenings of life and fly off to the moon. Eagle teaches you to follow the joy your heart desires. Do you understand?” The young, dark-brown complexioned man with coarse medium length black hair asked.

“Yes, very interesting. My name is Robin Mulvaina. So is this your first trip Atsa up to the moon?” asked Mulvaina

“Yes. My first trip. It is my own modern version of a Vision Quest. You know all natural objects within the universe have spirits. I hope to explore and meet the Moon Spirit. Then I will find out my purpose for this life. Do you understand?” The young man asked again.

“Yes, quite an ambitious goal Atsa, and quite innovative,

and also courageous on your part," answered Mulvaina.

Atsa raised his eyes and looked at Mulvaina, as if satisfied, he relaxed more into his seat.

Mulvaina closed his eyes. He felt a calmness coming over him, but it was suddenly interrupted by Atsa's voice in urgency. "Wow, Mulvaina, did you just see that gigantic, white, blinding flash of light. No noise. Just that gigantic flash. Did you see it?"

"No, what flash? I had my eyes closed," said Mulvaina.

"It was fantastic. It's a bizarre phenomena. There was a lecture I went to all about it. Scientists say the phenomena wreaks havoc on nearby computers and throws out higher levels of radiation. The flash has been nicknamed the Bermuda Triangle of Space. But don't worry, today's space rocket is resilient to the triangle's effect. Go ahead and rest."

"Oh, alright, I will," said Mulvaina. "I've got some things to think about." Mulvaina closed his eyes. As he was drifting in thought, he heard Atsa say, "Evolution has gone from ape to upright man to spacewalker. Stars are now just stepping stones from one space place to another."

"One place to another, one place to another. From Earth to the Moon, murder from one place to another," Mulvaina was trying to put the pieces together.

For four days Mulvaina sorted the data running through his mind. When he stepped into the entry port at the lunar base he still hadn't come to any conclusions, but he had several hunches, and one overriding longing and that was to see Julie. Even before he had surveyed the small crowd of waiting faces, Joe Grimaldi was approaching him. Mulvaina felt his heart sink just slightly then reminded himself that was totally the result of his own choosing. After all, he hadn't been absolutely sure he could make it up on the flight and so, he hadn't notified Julie. Oh well, he thought, surprising her was going to be much more fun. At least he hoped she would think so.

Grimaldi immediately had his hand out and was giving him a warm handshake. Mulvaina liked him, not just because of memories, but because of who and what Grimaldi was like in the present. He felt the man's genuine trustworthiness and bond of their friendship. "I'm sure glad you're stationed up here," Mulvaina said in greeting. "So what's been happening since I left Earth?"

"The contract's been awarded," said Grimaldi.

"Barish?" Mulvaina said more than asked.

"Seems NASA was so impressed with you being able to quickly reveal Dave Rodgers, or whatever his name was, that they felt everything was in order," answered Grimaldi.

"So everything went through?"

"Everything," said Grimaldi nodding affirmatively.

"Even the mineral rights to lunarcrete?" asked Mulvaina to be certain everything included the mineral rights.

"Yes, mineral rights, too," said Grimaldi.

"In general, how have things been going up here while I've been back on Earth?" Mulvaina asked.

"Things have become sort of strange. Jones and Farnsworth have been at each others' throats," answered Grimaldi.

"How do you mean?" Mulvaina asked refocusing his attention and energy as he could feel the sluggish effects of space travel.

"Well, in front of other staff, Farnsworth has been rudely admonishing Jones for writing reports that lunarcrete is falling below specifications," answered Grimaldi.

"Is that all?" Mulvaina asked pushing for more information.

"I overheard Farnsworth and Jones arguing over billings, too," continued Grimaldi. "It sounded like Farnsworth thought he was getting an improperly represented report which was shorting him some money. Also, Julie mentioned to me that she is worried about Jones because he never leaves his office. She says Jones even goes to sleep in his office. She's been bringing his meals to the office, too."

"Where's he bathing?" Mulvaina asked.

"Well," answered Grimaldi, "he does have an executive bathroom inside his office."

"I want to check something out. Let's stop by Jones' living quarters," said Mulvaina with urgency.

"What do you have in mind old buddy?" Grimaldi asked.

"You don't want to know," Mulvaina paused then added, "yet."

They turned down the living quarters corridor and went to the second to the last room on the right-hand side. The name plate on the door read... Fred Jones.

Mulvaina reached into his back pocket and took out a small brown leather covered case. He opened it and pulled out two small probe-like instruments and inserted them into the key hole. He pressed a button on the case and after a few seconds the door unlocked.

"Where do you buy one of those gadgets?" asked Grimaldi.

Mulvaina replied, "You didn't even see it or know that it exists."

The two men quickly entered the room. Mulvaina shut the door and felt for the light switch. The light glared on furniture turned upside down and over onto its sides, clothes scattered in a whirlwind mess, fragments of dishes lying between pages of open books, and a mattress slashed open and bleeding its foam stuffing across the pale tan carpet.

Grimaldi blew a deep low whistle. "I always thought Fred was a little neater housekeeper," he said sarcastically.

In my business this is known as a break-in and search," said Mulvaina.

"How can you be certain?" Grimaldi asked.

"Because whoever did this, did not seem to leave anything unturned," Mulvaina said.

"Why do you think Jones hasn't reported this?" asked Grimaldi.

"I don't know. Let's go ask him," answered Mulvaina.

As Mulvaina and Grimaldi were heading down towards the office corridor, Mulvaina slowed and looked at Grimaldi and asked, "How's Julie?"

"Fine. Under some pressure with this Jones' thing. I was

surprised she didn't meet you at the entry port," replied Grimaldi.

"She didn't know I was arriving. Go on and I'll catch up with you in a few minutes," said Mulvaina with a grin that spread wide across his face.

Mulvaina sneaked up to the office door where he knew he would find Julie. He peaked in. Julie's back was turned away from her desk. She was looking into a large bag that a very heavy, cosmetically perfect-faced woman was holding. Mulvaina recognized the woman. She had been aboard his space shuttle flight.

"I have to hurry and go over to my office and report in, but I want you to see this wonderful new line of lipsticks I've brought back. They're the latest fashion colors on Earth," the woman said.

"Let's have dinner together tonight and try all the samples. And for sure I'll take my favorite; a bottle of Forever Yours," said Julie.

Mulvaina crossed his fingers for luck and immediately admonished himself for being boyish and superstitious. Then, conjuring up a charming tone said, "Excuse me. Is that you Julie?"

Julie swung around in her chair. "Oh! Robin," she said in absolute delight.

"We'll have dinner another night, Julie," said the woman with an understanding smile. Then she walked past Mulvaina, gave him a quick sensuous wink, and disappeared into the corridor.

Julie slowly walked over to Mulvaina. "Oooooh," she whispered between her lips with seductive charm.

Mulvaina grabbed her tightly around the waist and drew her towards him. "You look so, so good," he said softly and then he pressed his lips hard against hers.

Abruptly, a siren screamed from the overhead ceiling demanding, without a moment's delay, obedience.

Julie pulled away from Mulvaina "Wait here," she said. She ran to Jones' office door and began knocking on it rapidly. "Please, come out. You must. There's an emergency. It's the construction warning signal. There must have been an accident. Please," she begged. But the door stood shut. Not so much as a murmuring reply came from within Jones' office. Julie shook her fist in anger and bewilderment. There was no time to stand around and plead with a man without reason. She ran back to Mulvaina and grabbed his hand and pulled him along with her as she raced out of the office and down the hallway corridor.

Through the corridor, in silent emergency, men and women all with hurried pace headed for the construction site. Many carried with them bottles of plasma and rolls of bandages and some carried stretchers. Mulvaina felt empty-handed and like an intrusive bystander. He also felt Julie's hand sweating profusely in the palm of his hand.

Soon they had rounded the corner and were facing the construction site. The metal doors were swung wide open and inside were the cries of pain and shock, confusing explanations and commanding emergency orders. Men were frantically pulling away concrete rubble and broken forms and shoring beams. Suddenly there was a husky scream of relief and a huge oxen-shaped man began to pull a worker out from underneath the rubble. Mulvaina flinched slightly as he saw the bleeding legs and the unsightly angle at which the legs dangled and the jagged bones that protruded from the anemic colored skin. Then came a deafening hush. The oxen-shaped man had pulled up the second trapped man and his body laid limp across his rescuer's arms. A medic rushed to their side and leaned down onto the victim's chest and then let out an exclamatory shout, "He's alive." A hundred sighs of relief and hope filled the air.

From out of the crowd Mulvaina saw the face of Joe Grimaldi coming into focus. Grimaldi carfully worked his way through the crowd. Soon he was at Mulvaina's side.

"A beam collapsed during tensioning," explained Grimaldi. "Ironically, the inspector was here. In fact, I understand from one of the carpenters that he was arguing with some of the construction workers about the quality of the work. The carpenter told me that just minutes before the beam collapsed, several of the men had a confrontation with the inspector. First, it was just some name calling like stupid asshole, etc., but then suddenly two men jumped

the inspector and worked him over pretty good. He has already
been taken to the base hospital."

Suddenly a shout went up. "There's another body." More
men rushed to the rubble site and dug frantically. Mulvaina could
see the bottom half of a torso sticking out from a huge massive
slab of concrete. "Only a miracle could bring that man back to
life," he uttered under his breath.

Julie buried her face against Mulvaina's chest. He felt her
whole body shaking. Mulvaina put his arm around her to hold her
in place so she wouldn't see what was next.

"Shit," said Grimaldi stunned. "He's been decapitated."

Mulvaina felt very sick. An hour later when he was back in
his living quarters' room, he threw up his late morning breakfast.
After he showered, he went over to check on Julie. When she
opened the door he saw her eyes had aged tremendously. Some
silly boyhood saying came spurting out of his mouth. "You never
feel so good as you do after you throw up," he said.

Tears began running down Julie's face. "Stay with me
tonight," she said. "Please, stay. And just hold me all night."

CHAPTER 21

Mulvaina stood in the living quarters' hallway studying the array of black and white photographic moonscapes. "Vistas without parallel," he said to Julie who was standing by his side.

"Our moon is incredible," she replied.

"What do York's photographs say?" said Mulvaina, thinking aloud.

"Say?" questioned Julie. "Why Charles York's photos give mankind a truthful reproduction of the moon," she said.

"Reality is colorful, not shades of gray," said Mulvaina in a contemplative tone. Then after a few moments he added, "York's work is excellent. These, here in the living quarters' hallway, show the man's perception, intuition, imagination and mechanical skill. They are reproductions with emotional impact. They are art. But the ones in the excavation site office, well, they lack energy and an appeal to the mind. They are simply black and white," Mulvaina paused, "simply," he stopped and looked at Julie all the while his mind was formulating the correct word, "simply documents. Yes, that's it, nothing more than documents."

Julie smiled in acknowledgment but without insight into Mulvaina's direction of thought. "Should we get breakfast now?" she asked.

"Yes, of course," said Mulvaina.

They said very little to each other while they ate, but Mulvaina did note with what seemingly genuine affection Julie buttered a piece of toast, spread strawberry jam across it, and then handed it to him. He felt more and more as if he belonged with her in a way that said he always had and always would.

After they had eaten, Julie fixed a breakfast tray of scrambled eggs and bacon and hot tea for Jones. "He really eats so little these days," she told Mulvaina as they headed for Jones' office.

Julie knocked respectively on Jones' office door. "Mr. Jones, I have your breakfast for you," she said.

"Coming," said a low muffled voice and then soon the door opened slightly. "What's Mulvaina doing here?" Jones asked gruffly.

"We had breakfast together this morning," Julie answered as she handed Jones the tray.

"You're working lots of overtime, uh?" inquired Mulvaina just as Jones was beginning to close the door.

"Might say that," answered Jones.

"I came across some information that may be of interest to you," said Mulvaina.

For a few seconds Jones seemed to stare right through Mulvaina. He then simply nodded his head in an affirmative manner and opened the door wider.

"I'll wait outside," Julie said with understanding.

Mulvaina stepped into the office. Jones shut the door and walked over to his desk and set the breakfast tray down. Mulvaina distinctively heard the absence of a lock's click. The man, he thought, was either very tired and off his guard or not quite as paranoid as Grimaldi and Julie suggested. "Please, eat your breakfast while we talk. It's probably already on the cool side. It's a little distance from the cafeteria to your office," said Mulvaina.

Jones picked up the coffee mug. "What information do you have that you think might interest me?" Jones asked.

"Your living quarters have been ransacked," Mulvaina said without emotion.

Jones acted unsurprised. "That's one of the problems of having the living quarters off the security surveillance," he said.

"In my professional opinion, the search was unsuccessful," said Mulvaina.

Jones picked up a piece of bacon, took a bite and chewed with his mouth slightly open. "Man is a hungry wolf," said Jones.

"Is that an accurate description of Mr. Farnsworth or do you see him as one of the new radical commercializers of space?" asked Mulvaina.

Then, suddenly as if Mulvaina had the power to summon the very devil himself, the door swung open, Julie was hollering, "He's not available, please stop," and in walked Farnsworth with what seemed to Mulvaina as an air of evil intent.

Upon seeing Mulvaina, Farnsworth shifted moods as smoothly as an actor, and burst into a flamboyant smile. "Mulvaina. I caught a glimpse of you at the construction site accident. Needless to say, I was too occupied to get over and welcome you back. I'll tell Rachel you're here and we'll get together for dinner, possibly tomorrow night," he said.

"Thank you. I appreciate the offer and look forward to it," said Mulvaina.

"I'm sorry that I interrupted you and Fred. I have something urgent to discuss with him about yesterday's accident. Would you excuse us for a few minutes," Farnsworth tone was a definite one of command.

"It's alright. Mulvaina can stay," Jones said quickly before Mulvaina could answer.

Mulvaina felt caught in the men's tug-a-war. Did Jones seem afraid to be in the room alone with Farnsworth? Possibly. But Mulvaina weighed the probability of foul play while he was going to be present in the next room and dismissed it as highly unlikely. He settled the struggle and said, "I'll just wait outside. I have something I need to take care of with Julie anyhow." Mulvaina left the room. He felt an uneasiness perhaps caused, he reasoned, by Jones' anxiety.

Julie looked up from the small computer monitor she held in her hand as Mulvaina came out and shut Jones's office door behind him. "Mr. Jones is going to be so angry at me. Mr. Farnsworth was absolutely on his 'no see' list," she said.

"Do you have any idea why?" asked Mulvaina.

"That was one of the first orders Jones gave me when he began locking himself up in his office last week," she replied.

"Do you think it has to do with a breach in quality control?"

"Heaven knows," said Julie. "Mr. Farnsworth has been in quite a disagreeable mood. Office gossip is that his wife is seeing someone else."

"Well, you certainly don't think she's seeing Jones. Do you?" asked Mulvaina surprised by Julie's office gossip.

"I don't think so. I mean as long as I've been here at the lunar base I've known that Mrs. Farnsworth and Mr. Jones were personally very friendly to each other. But I've never observed or felt it was anything romantic. I asked around. You know how curiosity is? It seems that Mr. Jones has worked for a long time with Barish International and is a close, trusted employee and friend to Mr. Barish and his family. Let's finish talking in my office," Julie said.

Mulvaina followed Julie the few steps over to her office. Once inside he continued his questioning. "Did Jones work for Barish International when Rachael was married to her first husband, Roderick Fellows?" asked Mulvaina.

"Must have," answered Julie. Then she added, "He has worked for the company they say for over twenty years. I think if there is anyone that Mr. Barish trusts it must be Fred Jones. Mr. Barish has given Mr. Jones a lot of authority and latitude in making decisions that hasn't been given to other supervisors of Barish International."

"Well, how would you know that? Is my Julie an undercover agent?" asked Mulvaina with good humor.

"No," said Julie seriously. "But when I talk to other supervisors' secretaries I've found out that I don't have to do all the red tape paper work for requisitions and the like which seems to be standard procedures for other sections of the company."

"Maybe things are just done differently on the moon," Mulvaina suggested.

"Possibly. But my intuition says it's due to the special position Mr. Jones has with the Barish family," said Julie with confidence in her reasoning.

Suddenly a loud deafening buzzer filled the room. Instantly, the entrance door of Julie's office slid shut. Mulvaina remembered the sound. "Where's the EDISUBS?" he asked trying to control the panic he felt swelling up inside him.

Julie pulled two out from a compartment in the side wall.

"What about Farnsworth and Jones?" Mulvaina asked.

"Don't worry. There are several EDISUB bags in Mr. Jones' office if his office is affected," answered Julie.

Mulvaina quickly grabbed the oxygen bottle from one and said, "Woops, I guess one of the bags isn't working again, we'll just have to share."

"I don't mind, but the gossip will be like wildfire once the rescue crews pick us up," said Julie with a warm smile.

"And here they come," said Mulvaina.

....

In the middle of the lunar day, with the sun nearly overhead but slightly off-set from the Earth, the main disk of the Earth appeared dark and yet its perimeter was a glowing ring. Mulvaina felt on one hand like a god and on the other hand like an amoeba in the grandeur of the cosmos.

The shadows were nearly vertical and sharp and distinct upon the moon's surface. Grimaldi tapped him on the shoulder. Mulvaina maneuvered in his space suit with difficulty, but at last was facing him. In the visor of Grimaldi's face plate, Mulvaina could see himself looking like a giant marshmallow man.

Grimaldi motioned Mulvaina to follow. They walked along the outside of the original permanent lunar structure which housed the administrative staff's offices. When they were near Jones' office, Grimaldi stopped and began to look carefully at the exterior duct pipes. Soon after following the lines for several feet, he paused and pointed at a specific line.

Immediately, Mulvaina saw the rupture in the pipe. "What

does this mean?" he asked.

Grimaldi replied, "It's the air recirculation line to Jones' office. We've been using these lines here and on our other space stations for years and I've never heard of one rupturing like this."

"Maybe it isn't due to material stress weakness," said Mulvaina.

"My thoughts exactly," said Grimaldi.

"Do you see any footprints out here from anyone that might have been here earlier?" asked Mulvaina as he looked down at the lunar surface. "Shit. There's hundreds," he said in naïve surprise.

"Footprints can last thousands of years up here," said Grimaldi.

"Makes a detective's job a little harder," said Mulvaina.

"Yes, old buddy, you might start to follow footprints and find your suspect is one of the original Apollo astronauts."

Mulvaina thought about laughing but found his space suit inhibiting. He let the thought escape in the rising of his eyebrows.

CHAPTER 22

"What do you think of Rachael?" Mulvaina asked Grimaldi as they hurried down the corridor towards Farnsworth's lab.

"She has a few loose ends," Grimaldi answered, "but," he added, "what she lacks in brains the gal makes up for in looks."

"Did you ever meet her first husband?" asked Mulvaina.

"No. But I hear he would have liked to kill Rachael," answered Grimaldi sarcastically.

"Ever heard any rumors why?" asked Mulvaina.

"Not really. Maybe jealousy. Her money may have attracted gigolos, gypsies, or Russian spys."

"Ummm." Mulvaina mulled over all the information piecing itself together in his mind.

When they reached the lab, the door was ajar. An uneasy feeling came over Mulvaina. He closed his eyes for a second. He saw nothing.

Grimaldi stepped in without caution and was immediately saying, "Farnsworth sure in the hell isn't here. Maybe he's back at his quarters."

Mulvaina surveyed the empty lab. "What's that sound?" Mulvaina asked.

"The solar furnace is on," answered Grimaldi. "The vacuum pumps are pulling out gassing from the chamber."

"It's operating then," Mulvaina said more as a point of statement rather than a question. He looked to the far left corner where there stood a computer terminal. The sight of it suddenly conjured up an old instinct that made him want to cower from it. Mulvaina took a deep breath and stepped forward out of the shadowy feeling. He became determined, with an old valor that would have beheaded serpents, killed dragons, turned back armies and dissolved enchantments, to face whatever it was head on.

"Operating but that's strange," Grimaldi said in an uneasy tone, "the feed belt has stopped."

Grimaldi quickly walked over to a video unit at the computer terminal. He looked down into the screen's view just for a second. "Christ," he stammered out as he quickly turned away.

"What is it?" Mulvaina asked as he rushed towards Grimaldi. When he looked at the screen, only his long detective experience of seeing brutal realities kept him from gasping in horror.

"Do you think the remains are those of Farnsworth?" Grimaldi asked.

"I believe so," answered Mulvaina. "I saw a pair of broken glasses off to the edge of the burning remains. They're just beginning to melt, but they look like the pair Farnsworth wears." Mulvaina corrected himself. "Wore."

CHAPTER 23

"Suppose Grimaldi you wanted to kill your wife and when you tried, you botched the whole thing and killed the maid instead. Suppose you went underground and changed your appearance, and then came back to try murdering your wife again. Who besides her would you also want to murder?" asked Mulvaina.

"Her new husband, I suppose," answered Grimaldi spontaneously.

"Exactly," said Mulvaina.

"Robin are you suggesting Roderick Fellows is on the moon? I mean how? Who? Wouldn't the Astro-Four someway detect him?"

"It didn't catch that Dave Rodgers was an imposter; that he wasn't part of the space shuttle crew, but an escaped convicted mob-enforcer. Once a person has developed an identity, it identifies the person as such. Astro-Four can't detect people with false identities I don't think," replied Mulvaina.

"Do you suspect anyone?" asked Grimaldi.

"Charles York, the photographer," Mulvaina stated.

"York! Why him?" asked Grimaldi surprised.

"He seemed to be making himself a trusted friend of Farnsworth. And, from what the gossip tells me, he also was spending more and more time developing a close friendship with Rachel. There's this nagging detail also that bothers me."

"And what is that?" asked Grimaldi.

"Fellows was an amateur photographer. I'm not positive, but it's definitely a path of thinking that I need to follow down a while."

"So what's your next step?"

"York's quarter," answered Mulvaina.

"I'm with you," said Grimaldi with understanding that danger was in the shadows.

No one answered Charles York's bell. Mulvaina tried the door knob. The door opened. The two men stepped inside. "Hello. Anyone home?" Mulvaina called.

"Now what?" asked Grimaldi.

"I'm not quite sure what I'm looking for. A clue of some type. Some personal habit detail. Something that betrays a person like a gray hair betrays a man that thinks he is still twenty," answered Mulvaina.

"I know what you mean," said Grimaldi. He walked over to the coat closet and started rummaging through its contents.

Mulvaina went over to a large black plastic utility closet and opened it. Stacked in neat layers, row upon row, photographs rested face down. Mulvaina began to systematically turn them up, one by one. The first four shelves held black and white photo upon photo of a pocked moon surface at varying tilting angles of the camera or various curious views of the photographer's mind. Mulvaina only glanced at each briefly. He once again admitted to himself that the man exhibited a strong creative talent. No one ever said Fellows was anything more than an amateur or even possibly a pervert with a camera. On the fifth shelf Mulvaina found a selection of color photos of a display of orange and green volcanic glass beads. He looked at the photos, thought, then decided that simply the nature of the material had required York to choose colored film. He thumbed through a couple dozen more photos and then found himself bending down uncomfortably to search the bottom rows of the closet. He picked up a photo that showed a gray moon surface with a muted red-white-and blue flag that seemed like it was flapping in a vapor of wind. There were footsteps around it. In the background was the unmistakable form of the bottom stage of the Apollo Eagle lander. And in Mulvaina's mind came back those historic famous words that every child in America had memorized by age five, "One small step for man, one giant leap for mankind." He thought about it. The photo had definite creative spirit. Perhaps he was on the wrong track. He stood up deciding to check under the bed mattress, but something drew his eye back to the bottom and last shelf. Perhaps it was his detail for being meticulous, perhaps some inner vision, at any rate, Mulvaina bent down once more and began turning the last photos over. Suddenly, he let out a long, low whistle. He began turning photos over quickly and excitedly. His mind rushed forward making great leaps.

Grimaldi came up behind Mulvaina. "What did you find?" he asked.

"A different path," replied Mulvaina, "and the right one, I believe." Mulvaina spread out a half dozen photos the way a man lays out his poker cards when he knows he's won.

The photos were all candid shots of people living on the Lunar Base Camp. Mulvaina drew out one photo from the rest and handed it to Grimaldi. "I think this must have been taken with a telescopic lens. No one would let you stand on top of them and take such a revealing shot," Mulvaina said.

"It's Farnsworth whispering something to Dave Rogers," Grimaldi said in astonishment. "And," he added, "handing him something. It looks like money. Yes, he's handing him money."

Mulvaina thought aloud. "All the arguing. Locking himself up in his office. It's beginning to fit."

It was a moment or two before Grimald took in what he was hearing. Then he said in a crisp, sharp voice, "Jones."

•••••••••••••••••••••••••••••••••••••••

Mulvaina and Grimaldi found Julie typing a memo as they entered her office. Julie looked up efficiently, but her expression immediately turned to surprise. "What is it?" she asked anxiously.

"Where's Jones? Is anyone with him?" asked Mulvaina in rapid fire fashion. He could see he was upsetting Julie, but time he knew was running too short for greetings or a long explanation of the past hour's unraveling events.

"In his office. Why are you so breathless?" Julie asked nervously.

Mulvaina did not have a chance to answer. Suddenly, two gun shots echoed loudly. "No. No! We're too late," shouted Mulvaina.

Her hands shaking, Julie fumbled in her desk top drawer for the door key. She dropped it as she pulled it out. In one continuous movement, Mulvaina scooped it up off the floor, ran to Jones' office, jammed it into the key hole and instantly was thrusting the door wide open.

Jones' body was slumped back over his chair limply. Blood gushed from his mouth and nose and out his left eye. His white shirt was soaking blood. In his right hand, Jones held in a death grip a key shaped paperweight.

Mulvaina grabbed Julie just as she began to fall backwards. He leaned her head forward. "Take a deep breath, honey. A deep breath. Stay with me. I need you to call for emergency."

She heard his voice. Drew his strength. She pulled herself back from the swirling darkness and went over to Jones' intercom button on the wall. "Medical. Urgent," she said in a shocked but calm voice.

Grimaldi had laid Jones down on the floor and was holding his head turned sideways. "He's chocking on his own blood. His eye is filling with blood and it's oozing out, but I think the eye can be saved." With his left hand Grimaldi was putting pressure against Jones' chest. "His chest, though, took two direct hits. Where in the shit are those medics," Grimaldi said raising his voice.

Mulvaina leaned down close to Jones. "Who?" he asked in a whisper. Now he could barely feel Jones' pulse. "Who?" he shouted. "Whooooo," he screamed as a last resort knowing for Jones the medics would wheel him down the lighted tunnel singing songs of hosannas and Farnsworth would come to greet him and together they would watch the rest of the world, moon and universe from an entirely different perspective. Mulvaina took the key shaped paperweight out of Jones death grip and let the man's fingers rest in peace.

Once within his own clutch, Mulvaina suddenly realized the key shaped paperweight was exactly the same as the one that had been presented to him that very first time he left the lunar base.

CHAPTER 24

The medics did come. They said they would take the body directly to the coroner's small room inside the base hospital. "Obvious is obvious," said one medic.

"Everyone is only one heartbeat away from death," said another as if explaining a philosophical principal.

"He was gone before you received the call," reassured Mulvaina. Hell why had he even bothered to say that he wondered. The medics callousness made them less human than robots. After they had sacked the body and wheeled it out, Mulvaina called to Julie.

She came into Jones' office timidly. Mulvaina noticed she was shivering. He left Grimaldi's side and walked over to her. Julie threw her slender arms around his upper body and buried her face in his chest. She began to sob silently.

For a few moments it seemed to Mulvaina that all of them hung in some timeless, spaceless void that was neither moon nor Earth nor light or dark, neither warm or cold, nor moving or still. He felt like the three of them were in a photograph, perhaps captured by York's skillful eye, perhaps already hanging on the living quarters' hallway corridor wall and being observed at this very moment. Jones' killer might even be commenting, "How melodramatic of a scene. Or how romantic," Mulvaina thought.

It was Julie, herself, that broke the still-life picture. "Who would have done such a thing to poor Mr. Jones?"

"Who, indeed," said Mulvaina. "It had to be someone who had access to this office through another entrance. Does that back door to the bathroom lead to an outside corridor?"

"Why indirectly, yes, it does," replied Julie. "If you were coming from the corridor, you would still need Jones' key to the office to open the bathroom door. From the bathroom you need the key to get inside the office. Jones always said it was a great idea. A double locking entrance." Then in a sudden gush of tears, Julie's face was flooded.

"What did you think of just now, Julie?" asked Mulvaina tenderly.

"Once Jones told me double locks weren't as good as my guard-dog stance! He said that one side of his flank was always safe as long as I was on duty." She wiped the tears away.

" Ummm," thought Mulvaina aloud.

"What?" asked Grimaldi.

"Jones must have had some doubt about the reliability of the Astro-Four System to detect intruders or…."

"Ms. Anderson," came a bellowing voice from outside the office room.

"In here," hollered Grimaldi.

Two security personnel entered Jones' office. One was short and overweight. One was too tall and too thin. Mulvaina had a fleeting thought that they presented the comic relief in a somewhat Greek tragedy. Of course, in his passing comparison he noted Jones was no great hero, possibly only a minor character. Or was Jones perhaps more?

The too tall, too thin man interrupted Mulvaina's reflective efforts to a conclusion. "Did you see anyone enter into Mr. Jones' office, Ms. Anderson?" he asked.

"No. No one. He's…" She stopped. She started again. "He had been alone for several hours."

"Didn't your monitors show who came into the office with Mr. Jones?" asked Mulvaina almost already knowing the answer.

"Our monitors showed that no one was with Mr. Jones," the too tall, too thin man answered.

"But that's impossible, we were here when the shots were fired. Someone came through that back door. Someone killed him," bellowed Grimaldi infuriated at what he felt was either incompetency, stupidity, or impossibility.

In quick bursts of three, the phone rang at Jones' desk.

Julie answered it. "It's for you," she said handing the receiver to the short, fat security man.

"Yes. It was? Yes, I'll tell Mr. Mulvaina. They have? Fine, I'll tell him that, too." The security man hung the phone up and turned to Mulvaina. "The body in the solar furnace has been identified as that of John Farnsworth. A physician and security man have been sent to Mrs. Farnsworth's to notify her and protect her if necessary."

"Have they removed the remains of the body from the furnace?" asked Mulvaina.

"Yes. The remains are in the security storage room. We'll give you protection down to there now," answered the security man.

"Protection," said Mulvaina. The years had taught him that his only protection was his own instinct, his own reliance and strength. However, he let the offer stand unchallenged and said merely, "Thank you."

It was not an easy thing to do, but Mulvaina reached into the box holding Farnsworth's remains and picked up the metal glob that had been next to his body in the furnace. It mechanically had been scooped up and was still with the remains. "What kind of metal is this?" he asked the security men.

"It looks familiar, like brass, maybe," said the one that was too tall and too thin.

"Like metal they make keys from" inquired Mulvaina.

"Yeah, sure, maybe," said the man that was too short and overweight.

Mulvaina's mind flashed back to Jones' office room. Jones' body was slumped back over his chair. Blood gushing from his face. Blood soaking shirt. And in his right hand, a paperweight shaped like a key; a death grip upon it. Mulvaina's mind flashed further back. He was receiving recognition, a moon present, a paperweight shaped key from Jones as a remembrance of his first trip to the moon and Lunar Base Camp. "When does the next shuttle leave for Earth?" Mulvaina asked.

The tall security guard looked at his watch. "In about six

hours. Why? Are you ready to return to Earth so soon?" he asked.

"There isn't much more that I can do here. It's really a matter for your own security people. I better get back to Earth and see if I can sort things out. Distance can make the heart grow fonder. It can also make the mind become a little more focused. Distance can make the key to these deaths stand out like a dark night can make the stars shine bright," Mulvaina said, knowing all too well that he must get back as quickly as possible because the key to solving the case was indeed truly on Earth.

CHAPTER 25

The shuttle waiting room was like something out of the past. A disorderly, shoving, pushing herd of people were lining up in front of the port's entrance gate. The room carried loud voices but they swarmed together like angry bees. Indeed, no matter how well trained, no matter how well acclimated to the moon, no matter how far removed from Earth, these loud voices all belonged to the homo sapiens of the world. There was an invisible umbilical cord that attached them all still to original sin and to the first violence of Cain and Able. Mulvaina at the moment felt the pain of understanding that man had gained so little. Maybe perhaps even nothing, he thought as he took in the waiting room scene. Suddenly, he caught a glimpse of Mrs. Farnsworth flanked by security guards, meandering her way through the crowd and up to the front of the line. One of the security men held a square wooden box, almost like an old fashioned hat box, but not so deep, that surely kept the remains of John Farnsworth. A bouncing curvaceous figure with thick, long brown hair went running up to Mrs. Farnsworth and thrust herself into the other's arms. She wailed, "Oh my God they killed John. Not John. Oh my God." Then like a wounded creature she thrashed her head and shrieked an ancient death moan.

Mulvaina observed Rachael's complete self-control. He wondered, was it shock? Was it breed? Was it simply training in social grace? Was it civilization? Or was it satisfaction? Mulvaina really wasn't quite sure at the present. Then shouting burst through the room breaking his thoughts.

"Make way. Make way." The medical were wheeling the sacked body of Fred Jones towards the front of the line.

Mulvaina pushed himself forward and forward into the

crowd until at last he came to Grimaldi and Julie. "Looks like the whole the Lunar Base Camp is intent on going home to Earth," he said.

"Everyone is a little jumpy over the murders. I guess if they had an excuse to go back and could get clearance, they're heading out to guarantee they are not the next victim of whatever madman is roaming the base! How did you get priority so quick anyhow, Robin?" Grimaldi asked.

"Security granted it. I stroked their ego some. I said they could handle everything and I really needed to get back to handle some matters on Earth."

"And you?" asked Mulvaina.

"NASA demanded my immediate return with all my confidential records on current operations. I do believe they are possibly worried the murders are the beginning of something bigger, maybe even sabotage of the base," said Grimaldi. Then he asked, "And how did the two of us luck out to have you, Miss Julie, to accompany us back on the long flight home?"

"Mr. Barish, himself, ordered my priority. He wanted me to bring back all the personal files I keep and present them to the corporation's top executives. He also ordered Rachael to come right home so she would, of course, be assured her safety. Mr. Barish said he would be sending his son up to take over and head the base on the shuttle's return trip up. But get this. Rachel is refusing to go back. She's here just boarding her husband's remains. She says she is a Barish and just as capable as her brother and that the business is her life and her responsibility," Julie paused. Then she added, "Also Rachael says she intends to stay and manage things not only now, but on an equal basis when her brother comes. Can you beat that? If I was her, I would be scared as hell that I would be the next victim. She's more gutsy than I ever realized. I thought she was more into her appearance and social calendar. I'll tell you, Robin, I was never so ready to leave a place in all my life. After what happened in Jones' office, I just don't feel safe at all here on Lunar B.C. I hardly can wait to get aboard the shuttle." Julie ended with a deep sigh.

Mulvaina smiled reassuringly but he felt a pang of guilt when Julie relaxed her anxious, tense stand and gave him a little girl smile, for he had a strong sense of danger and wouldn't feel safe until the shuttle landed and he planted his feet firmly on Earth.

....

Rachael Farnsworth was the first one to leave the waiting room and enter the shuttle cabin. Security held back the other passengers, but at that moment it really was a perfunctory gesture as the room fell silent. It even seemed to Mulvaina that most of the lunar base personnel lowered their heads as Mrs. Farnsworth carried her small wooden box through the port door and into the shuttle cabin. The atmosphere, he thought, was very similar to family and friends standing at the grave's side. He wondered for just a moment if John Farnsworth's killer might also be standing unobtrusively in this very same waiting room also waiting to board the shuttle.

Soon Rachael came walking slowly through the port door once again. Her self-control was shaken slightly and a few maverick tears ran down her cheeks. When she reached the first security guard, he took her by the forearm and began to lead her off to the side of the crowding line. The other guards stepped aside and the line began to rush forward and head for the shuttle. When Mulvaina was close to where Rachael stood, he stepped out of line and approached her. "Mrs. Farnsworth," he said as he extended his right hand, which she immediately took and clasped hers over, "I am so sorry about this tragic death of your husband. I feel partially responsible for your grief in the fact that I failed to find and stop his killer in time. But I assure you, I will not rest until the authorities have arrested his murderer."

"You did what you could. This, Mr. Mulvaina, makes so very little sense to me. It's such a waste of such a good, fine man."

"Are you sure it is wise for you to remain here at Lunar

Base Camp?" Mulvaina asked. "I don't want to alarm you, and certainly you will have top security surrounding you day and night, but the killer of your husband and probably Mr. Jones is obviously a very clever person who has been able to somehow evade the Astro-Four System. By staying, you are putting yourself at a risk. Couldn't I talk you into taking this shuttle back home with me."

"I am Barish International. I will stay," Rachel stated coldly. And then, she added with very definite conviction, "I will be safe."

"Of course," said Mulvaina in a sympathetic manner. He noticed that Rachael's self-control was very much back in place. Maybe staying and keeping busy would be better for her than sitting strapped down for days in the shuttle where she could only think and grieve. Instinct knew best. And sometimes Mulvaina reminded himself, survival was synonymous with instinct

"Have a pleasant trip back and do rest in peace," said Rachael and then she turned and led herself and her guard away.

"Rest in peace." Rachael's words resounded in Mulvaina's mind. She must have meant get some rest, or rest in peace that she would be safe, or….Mulvaina let the thought drop as Grimaldi and Julie came up behind him.

"Come on old buddy," Grimaldi said. "Let's board this shuttle and get some rest for a few days."

Mulvaina really had not realized he was so exhausted. He found that he indeed needed rest and lots of it. He slept through most of the shuttle's journey through its trail of stars. On the last day of the trip, he felt fresh and energetic. He looked over at Julie who was still dozing with a sweet angelic look upon her face and he also felt very much in love. Now he was getting anxious to get to Earth and not only plant his feet on solid ground, but also have a chance to wine and dine Julie and see some of the world with her.

"Robin." Grimaldi's voice got Mulvaina's attention. "It's more than just the fact that Farnsworth is dead."

"Yes, I was wondering about the future of the company too," answered Mulvania. "What happens to Lunarcrete now?"

"Control of the company goes over to his widow, Rachael,"

said Grimaldi.

"And the mineral rights?" asked Mulvaina. "What about them?"

"It's not exactly clear. I think the rights can either stay with Rachael or return to the prime contractor which, of course, is Barish," answered Grimaldi.

"I see," said Mulvaina. "It really makes little difference, they are essentially the same. So how much longer to re-entry?"

"Should be quick now," answered Grimaldi. He looked down at his watch. "Matter of fact," he added, "they should have already released the freight pods."

"Yeah," said Mulvaina. He looked down at his watch. A perplexed frown spread across his face and darkened his skin with anxiety. "I didn't hear the call. Did you?"

Joe Grimaldi leaned across both Mulvaina and Julie and looked out the shuttle's side portal. The approaching Earth nearly filled the entire half of the window's view.

Mulvaina immediately noticed that worry shadowed Grimaldi's face. He raised his eyebrows. It was his way of telling Grimaldi he was worried, too.

Grimaldi unstrapped his safety belt, got up out of his seat, walked across the aisle, leaned across a few sleeping passengers, and looked out several of the other side portals. He turned back towards his seat and when his eyes met Mulvaina's eyes there was instant understanding between the two men that there was definitely something very wrong. Grimaldi sat back into his seat and whispered to Mulvaina, "Let Julie keep sleeping." Then, he added, "We are much too close to re-entry to still be in this altitude." Grimaldi pressed the attendant-wanted button on the overhead shuttle ceiling and the button turned green. In a few seconds, a thin, young male attendant came walking down the aisle and stopped at Grimaldi's seat.

"Yes, Colonel Grimaldi is there something I can get you?" the attendant asked pleasantly.

"Is the shuttle having any kind of mechanical problem that the pilot hasn't notified the passengers about?" asked Grimaldi in a calm but commanding voice.

The attendant looked puzzled. "No, nothing," he said genuinely. Then almost as an after-thought, he mentioned casually, "In fact, everything has been nice and quiet and rather slow and easy for us attendants. We haven't even had a coffee request from the pilot for several hours now."

Mulvaina could feel Grimaldi's alarm it was so intense. And when Grimaldi stood right up, Mulvaina glanced for a second at Julie and was grateful she was still sleeping, then immediately stood up and was ready to follow his friend to the cockpit. Mulvaina's first thought was piracy, his second was hijacking, and his instinct suggesting the third alternative made him say a quick prayer for deliverance from evil.

"Let's go up and say hello to that pilot and make sure he's not napping on the job and letting auto-pilot do more than its job," said Grimaldi to the attendant.

The attendant smiled and laughed lightly. "Of course, Colonel Grimaldi, the command crew will be pleased to see you and I can check to see if they're ready for a cup of coffee."

The attendant led the way up the aisle. When he reached the cockpit door, he knocked softly. "Captain Stewart, sir. Colonel Grimaldi would like to come up front and say hello."

Grimaldi counted, "One. Two. Three." There was no reply. None, from within the cockpit. In one sweeping movement, Grimaldi pushed the attendant to the side. He pulled on the door. It was not locked. He quickly swung open the cockpit door.

CHAPTER 26

George Carver pushed his chair away from the desk, stood up erect, and faced the back wall of his office. He recalled his army boot camp days and the hours of disciplined standing tall and straight in the hot California summer air. It was a time when he was new off the L.A. streets and had enough energy it seemed to run across America with barely stopping to take a breath. At eighteen he had joined the army. He had been stirred to patriotic duty from the nightly news as it was broadcasted against the softly orchestrated Star-Spangled Banner. News, intense with spy photos from a multitude of drones world-wide that had replaced all U-2 and SR-71 spy planes. News with columns of steel armored fighting tanks, marching armies upon marching armies, blood soaked massacres, fire-line executions, gruesome beheadings, that flashed upon the screen. Flashes, that were like distant lightening before the devastating storm overhead. And the bombardment of this nightly news aroused within him all human yearnings for freedom, democracy and civil rights. His youthful bravery was ready. His manly strength was fully awake. The antiquated dragon had come forth breathing gusts of fire in rampage across the world. He would be one of the many young men that would prepare to be a dragon slayer.

In those youthful days, Carver recalled dreaming of heroic glory. While many of his army buddies did only what was demanded of them, he spent his extra time studying the history of the world, especially its great wars and its great military leaders. He admired the ancient wisdom of General Patton. He read and re-read Patton's principles nightly as he laid in his bunk bed exhausted from the long-day of realistic training experiences that were ment to ensure his success on the battlefield. He had been fascinated by Patton's premise that brains came from oxygen, oxygen came from the lungs, and that if a person could double their lung power then a person could be twice as smart, and that in the long run of things it was brains not savagery that won wars.

On his off time he had stood in that hot California sun and had not been idle. He had almost doubled his lung power during that six weeks of boot camp. Now as he faced his office wall, he breathe more air into his lungs, held it for a thirty second count, and then let it out ever so slowly. He did it again and again until he had taken ten deep breaths. Finished, Carver let his mind go over the facts. The FBI Intelligence Network was coming in with photos of prominent organized crime heads and known hit personnel in increasing numbers. It was obvious that L.A. county was becoming the hot get together spot and Carver knew it wasn't a reunion at the Long Beach Pike to take in the latest virtual reality rides. In fact, it was becoming clear that the mafia was putting together an entire assassination team. Someone was going to be eliminated because he knew something important that could stop a lot of bucks going into a lot of pockets.

The detail that Carver believed the most important to the mafia's course of action was the fact that Salvo's hospital room was guarded around the clock by one of their men. Salvo could obviously identify who invaded their secret desert facility. The head man was just waiting for Salvo to become conscious and sign the guy's death warrant. From intelligence reports of the rush of mafia coming into the county within the last seventy-two hours, Carver suspected some neurosurgeon must have suggested that Salvo would regain consciousness soon.

Carver took another deep breath. He said aloud to himself, "I'm going to get the enemy because I will be smarter than the enemy. Mafia are lazy breathers."

Carver also knew a very capable and pretty RN who worked at the third floor of the hospital where Salvo had his private intensive care room. She had the number to his personal cell and could get him anywhere, any time. She definitely would call him the minute Salvo opened his eyes and or opened his mouth to speak. In fact, Carver had no doubts about it, for the RN was not only pretty and sweet, but also FBI Intelligence. Yes, he assured himself, the enemy was his all in due time.

CHAPTER 27

"Shuttle 405. Shuttle 405, please reply. Give status. We are showing you at a dangerous altitude. Shuttle 405, please reply. We are not, I repeat, not read…you…," a radio voice stuttered with static and then died out.

Grimaldi heard the words even before he saw the slumped, unconscious figures in the cockpit. Intuitively, he surmised the shuttle had been sabotaged. "Gas," he hollered as he grabbed down two oxygen masks from the cockpit ceiling, quickly putting one on, and handing the other to Mulvaina.

Grimaldi reached for the pilot. Then the co-pilot. He shook his head in a manner that Mulvaina knew meant "dead". Simultaneously they lifted the bodies out of their seats and dropped them on the floor. Mulvaina quickly assumed co-pilot position. "Can you still fly one of these things?" he asked.

"Doesn't look like I've got any choice," answered Grimaldi. He looked out the window. Slowing air was passing by. "The shuttle is in re-entry and we sure as hell have a rotten altitude. A few more minutes like this and we'll be burning up."

Mulvaina noticed outside air glowed brighter by the second. He felt sweat running down his entire body. The cabin temperature was rising at an alarming rate. "Do something," he screamed at Grimaldi who seemed to be almost hypnotized by the panel as the instruments wildly flashed warning lights.

"You know Robin, I always wanted to see what it would be like to fire the main engines during re-entry. It was a maneuver that the computer simulation said might work, but, of course it was something we were not allowed to try."

Mulvaina grasped Grimaldi's tone of voice. At first he felt his whole body wanting to explode in panic, but then realizing death was most likely inevitable he succumbed to some sudden inner calm and peace. Perhaps, he thought, it was the calm a man reaches after he has jumped off a tall building and is in mid-air. Perhaps, it is the calm that comes from no longer fighting death. A calm that comes from complete acceptance.

"Here's to Geronimo!" said Grimaldi as he pushed the throttle forward.

CHAPTER 28

Carver's cell rang. He picked it up quickly and said "hello." It wasn't who he expected. The deep male voice took him by complete surprise. He refocused. "I'm sorry. Will you start again. I just heard the word shuttle and nothing more," Carver apologized.

"Sir, according to our data, Shuttle 405 should have been finished with re-entry ten minutes ago. It's possible they are having some kind of radio transmission difficulty, but I decided to notify you immediately because it had been mentioned to me that you are expecting some important passengers aboard the flight. I'll keep you posted. Wait. Wait Just a minute. My assistant is calling me over."

There was a break in the conversation, but Carver could still hear a distant scrambling of alarmed voices. After a few minutes the male voice was back and urgently explaining, "Pre-entry data is clearly showing that the shuttle was in an improper altitude at the moment contact was lost. Landing surveillance has had no sign of the shuttle. We must conclude that Shuttle 405 has been lost. We are now notifying the Air Force and Navy to begin searching for the wreckage. In just a few minutes our personnel will notify the space port so they can advise family and friends awaiting shuttle passengers. We hope the media vultures stay away for awhile so we have time to look for answers. I'll call you later as soon as we find out anything."

"Thank you. I appreciate the immediate call," said Carver. He hung up in disbelief. Almost instantaneously his cell rang again.

"Yes," Carver answered expecting additional information from the male voice. Again he was surprised. It was not the male voice but the voice of the hospital third floor RN.

"He's conscious and fingered your man," she stated quickly. Then the connection went dead.

It was all Carver needed to know, but now the vital information might only be excessive data in the tragic after news of the shuttle's fate. Before Carver could hold the thought, the cell suddenly rang again. "Hello," Carver answered anxiously.

"Sir, we have had contact with Shuttle 405."

Carver recognized the male voice. "Thank God," he blurted out in almost a shout.

The male voice continued, "The shuttle has declared 'Mayday, Mayday, Mayday. I stress the call was given three times in a row to prevent mistaking it for some similar-sounding phrase. There's a good chance it will land at the space port, off schedule but hopefully without much damage."

"What happened?" Carver asked.

"First, the shuttle entered wrong. That caused it to disappear from our screens. Besides that, it is not certain at this time what has been going on aboard the shuttle. But it is much more than mechanical difficulty. There is the possibility, sir, of sabotage. One thing for sure is the fact that Joe Grimaldi is now piloting Shuttle 405 for its landing."

"Grimaldi?" Carver said in surprise.

"Yes, sir. You heard that right."

"Talk to you later. I've got to move fast," said Carver.

"I understand," answered the male voice.

Carver ran out of his office. He knew he had to intercept the killers lying in wait for Mulvaina. Had the killers heard the newest shuttle information before they exited the space port? Or were they waiting somewhere else for the right moment to again surface and get their target. A wrong deduction Carter told himself would certainly mean the very death of Mulvaina.

CHAPTER 29

Anxious faces were bursting into joyful tears as passengers from Shuttle 405 walked into the space port. In a few moments the paralysis of politeness broke into a spontaneous rushing of people giving and receiving hugs and kisses. The minutes previously consumed by enormous fear of fatal consequences were replaced with an uncontrolled fever of excitement.

A large framed man suited in Mission Control attire planked by armed security rushed towards Grimaldi and Mulvaina just as the two stepped into the port. Mulvaina grabbed Julie's hand and drew her close to his side.

"Mission Control Chief," the large framed man stated with authority as security enveloped Grimaldi into their flanks and whisked him away.

Suddenly Mulvaina glimpsed Thomas Helms pushing his way forward. Holding Julie's hand firmly, Mulvaina also pushed forward to meet him. "We're up against a foe that can go undetected everywhere," Mulvaina said in a whispered greeting.

"The car is waiting right outside," answered Helms. Then, he nodded his head briefly acknowledging Julie. She smiled back but said nothing.

The walk to the car was hurried and silent. Mulvaina opened the back door for Julie and she slid in quickly. Mulvaina got into the front passenger seat. Helms punched a few programming buttons and the car car pulled out into the street and began dodging buses, taxies, and other cars, slowly edging its way along the passenger pick-up lane.

"I still don't understand how Jones was shot. The security system must either have broken down or someone tampered with it," said Mulvaina as if he was talking to himself and reasoning the problem aloud.

"I was talking with a friend of mine yesterday. Years ago he worked for Barish International," Helms said in an interrupting tone. "My friend was a computer program expert. He was one of the initial people that worked on the program for the Astro-Four System."

"Anything in the system that's not suppose to be there?" Mulvaina asked with perked interest.

"There is something all right, but it was intended to be there," answered Helms. "When my friend heard about all the shit happening on the moon, he decided it was time to breech company confidence and not hold his silence any longer. He told me that the company has a secret built-in program to ignore the presence of anyone wearing one of three special badges."

"And who has those badges?" asked Mulvaina.

"He didn't know. And I believe him. But my friend did say the badges were requested by John Barish and he personally gave them to Mr. Barish," explained Helms.

"A very interesting little piece of the puzzle," said Mulvaina just as the car turned into the MFP Associates driveway.

Mulvaina turned to the back seat and smiled at Julie. Her eyes were closed shut, but he could tell she was not sleeping. He wished he could shut his eyes for just a second of rest. The shuttle trip in and of itself was an exhausting event, but with the added harrowing incident of being co-pilot, he felt like he had waged battle with a vicious enemy. "Is there a hammer anywhere in the office?" he asked Helms.

"I think there is one in the utility closet. Are we hanging moonscape photos on the wall?" asked Helms with surprised humor.

"The paperweight Jones gave me as a souvenir," said Mulvaina.

Helms did not react to Mulvaina's indirect answer. Mulvaina turned around again to look at Julie. This time Julie's provocative eyes were open. "Lock the car when we get out, stretch out on the back seat, and get some sleep. It won't take us too long. We're just heading up to the office for a few minutes and then we will be back," Mulvaina told Julie

"Be very careful, please," Julie said.

Mulvaina wondered why she stressed the word "very". Did she sense something? He knew he felt a strong sense of danger. He considered ordering Helms to stay with Julie. He would never forgive himself if Helms became his human shield against the invisible foe. Helms had his wife, his daughter, his…but Mulvaina's deductions were too slow coming to conclusion. Helms was out of the car and already taking quick strides and was almost to the front office door. Mulvaina slammed his side of the car door shut and hurried to catch up. "Helms, let me go into the office first," hollered Mulvaina not really knowing why but feeling the necessity to give the direction.

Helms obeyed without hesitation or question. He stepped aside as Mulvaina put his key into the door lock and turned it clockwise. Mulvaina placed his right hand under his pant at the waistband at the 5 o'clock position. He released the safety on his gun. With his other hand, he swung the door open.

The office was empty. At one glance, everything seemed in order. "Clear," hollered Mulvaina. Helms walked in and then Mulvaina quickly shut and locked the door. Helms went to the utility closet and took out a hammer and brought it to Mulvaina.

Mulvania went over to his desk and picked up the lunarcrete paperweight key that Jones had given him. He placed the key on the floor and brought the hammer down in heavy blows. The noise of steel against lunarcrete reverberated through the room once, twice, and then suddenly with the third force of the hammer the paperweight became rubble pieces. Inside the rubble laid a key with a plastic tab and a small cylindrical vial with a slip of paper in it. Without a word, Mulvaina opened the vial and took out the slip of paper, then looked up at Helms and said, "An authorization signed by Fred Jones giving me permission to open his safety deposit box."

No more words were needed to explain. Helms understood in an instant. The two men rushed to the car explaining briefly to

Julie that they were heading to the bank's location listed on the slip of paper.

"I've never seen an authorization like this," a young teller at the safety deposit window stated, "but I'll call my managing supervisor."

The managing supervisor, a man in his early 60's, approached with an air that seemed to indicate he was ready to give Mulvaina a stern lecture on bank rules. When, however, he saw Jones' signature on the slip of paper, his hand went suddenly to his lips and his eyes asked Mulvaina about Jones' well-being.

"I'm sorry to have to tell you he is dead," Mulvaina said respectfully.

The man nodded. "He was a dear old friend. He came to me personally when he made the authorization for you, Mr. Mulvaina, to be able to get to the contents in his safety deposit box. Your name is on our card file for the box number. See," he said withdrawing a card from the catalogue box. "Under certain circumstances we still do banking using this hand-filed system instead of requesting a person slip their hand under the light for finger print identification. Like in this case, we did not have your fingerprints on file with our bank. I believe you, of course Mr. Mulvaina, but I must see some photo ID, please."

Mulvaina pulled out his wallet and showed his detective license that had what he always thought was a good resemblance of himself. He glanced towards the file card and could clearly see his name on it. "Jones was murdered," Mulvaina whispered to the managing supervisor. It seemed to Mulvaina that the man grew older in a moment. Without saying anymore, he led Mulvaina and Helms into the vault and to the safety deposit box. He put in his key and Mulvaina put in his, and in what seemed to Mulvaina perfect togetherness of motion, they turned the keys. The managing supervisor let Mulvaina pull out the box and then led them to a small cubby-like room instructing Mulvaina to call him when he was finished with his business.

Mulvaina placed the box on the small table inside and locked the cubby-room's door. He paused for a few seconds and then opened the narrow, grey steel box. Lying on the top, picture face-up, was a 3 x 5 photograph of the body of a man partially buried in dirt. Mulvaina handed the picture to Helms.

Next, Mulvaina took out of the box a folded sheet of blueprinted plans. He looked at them for just a second before he said, "Foundation plan for the Barish International office building. And look here, Helms, there is a red "X" on one of the footings with this note beside it "LOCATION OF RODERICK FELLOWS' BODY."

Mulvaina handed the blueprint to Helms. Next, he removed several pages of a typed statement. He read it quietly; just loud enough for Helms to hear.

"To whom it may concern: It is obvious now that I am dead. I may have died of natural causes but most likely I believe I shall leave this world a victim of a violent murder. I take with me in death a hideous truth that has so sculptured my actions in my lifetime that only your future prayers can hope to beg God's mercy and deliver me from eternal damnation. This hideous truth is that Rachael Barish and her father, John Barish, murdered Rachael's husband, Roderick Fellows and murdered Rachael's maid who was Fellow's lover. On the morning of June 5, 2020 my foreman, Carl Soots, while inspecting the progress of a new wing addition being constructed onto the Barish office building made the discovery of Fellows' body crudely buried under one of the footings that was scheduled to be poured with concrete that day. When I notified Mr. John Barish of the discovery, he offered me a choice of joining the bodies or assisting him in maintaining their secrecy, at, of course, a generous monetary lifetime benefit."

Mulvaina looked up at Helms. "I think it is time to pay an unexpected visit to Mr. Barish at his office."

Helms nodded in complete agreement.

CHAPTER 30

John Barish was alone at his desk muddled in his thoughts. Too much was happening too fast now. He felt old age stressing his processing of all the negative information coming in from the moon base. He could not keep focused on a solution. The inter-office telephone buzzer went off, its tone multiplying its volume in his head. He slammed down on the buzzer's button as if it were a pesky fly he could easily kill with a swift swat.

"Mr. Mulvaina is here to see you, Mr. Barish." His secretary's voice informed him.

"Send him right in," he answered.

Mulvaina walked briskly into the room. Mr. Barish interrupted his forward stride.

"Mr. Mulvaina, I assume you have come here to fill me in on the progress of your investigation?"

"You might say that, Mr. Barish. Yes, indeed. You might say that," Mulvaina repeated.

"Well, let me fill you in on something first, Mr. Mulvaina. Initially I was impressed with the way you found out about that Dave Rodgers fellow. It calmed a lot of fears and got us the contract for Phase II signed. But now," Barish paused just for a second, "but now my son-in-law is dead, my project manager is dead, and the whole moon project is up in turmoil. And you, Mr. Mulvaina, have been totally incapable of preventing any of this. In my eyes, Mr. Mulvaina, you have been a failure. A total and complete failure. And I can assure you, you will never again work for this company." Barish paused again for a brief second and then added, "But I assume you have some weak explanation. Well, you better make it short Mulvaina and then get out."

The last desperate Barish power play Mulvaina thought.

"My explanation, Mr. Barish, begins ten years ago when Roderick Fellows and his mistress, your daughter's maid, were murdered as they tried to run off together," stated Mulvaina calmly but strongly.

"What! How preposterous! The truth of all that was settled years ago. Just go down and check the police files," Barish retorted back.

"Unfortunately for you, Fred Jones and Carl Soots discovered the body of Roderick Fellows where it had been clumsily buried under the future footings of this building's wing addition," said Mulvaina.

"You are getting more and more outrageous now, Mulvaina," Barish raised his voice.

"Shall I go on?" asked Mulvaina.

"By all means," said Barish, then he added, "I am amused by your fiction script."

"You treated Fred Jones and Carl Soots like two of your most valued employees. You gave them high responsibilities thinking you had ultimate power, life and death over them. In return, Jones and Soots robbed, embezzled and cheated you out of hundreds of thousands of dollars. And you, Mr. Barish, didn't know what to do but turn the other way and ignore their larceny." Mulvaina was quite aware now that he had Mr. Barish's full attention. He continued, "Then came your new son-in-law, John Farnsworth. He was a brilliant but ambitious man. Too ambitious. You set him up to make lunarcrete for the moon project; but not only was he making concrete for moon projects, he was also mining and shipping back to Earth fuel grade tritium enriched ores which he sold through a mob financed front company, Southwest Nuclear Fuels."

"Farnsworth owned Southwest Nuclear," Barish said calmly.

"Yes, he did," answered Mulvaina. "We know a mob man named Salvo was working with Farnsworth. He was handling pick-up and delivery of moon materials and the cash exchange. We don't believe Salvo knew the real potential of the moon material except its usefulness to the energy industry, but Middle

Eastern terrorists got wind of what was being sold on the black market and knew the material was just what they needed to make a substantial dirty bomb that could spread radioactive material; not so much inflicting heavy casualties but causing great terror and disruption and making land and buildings unusable for a long period of time. High-level radioactive materials are found in nuclear power plants and nuclear weapons sites and on the moon. The ambitious Farnsworth, I believe, intended to just make some extra large bucks on the side by selling his enriched moon ores to energy companies for their nuclear power plants, but terrorists infiltrated his business dealings. Salvo may have been deceived, or maybe not, and may have sold and passed moon materials to terrorists, but we do not have a real confirmation on this at the present time."

Mulvaina watched as Barish took out a handkerchief from his pant pocket and wiped the sweat off his forehead.

"And where does this put us with the deaths of Jones and Soots?" asked Barish.

"Jones and Soots knew Farnsworth was doing something clandestine but when Soots got too close to the truth, Farnsworth had him killed. After Soots' murder, Jones was in constant fear for his life while Farnsworth maneuvered to get from him the key that would unlock the entire Barish fortune, and allow him to operate Southwest Nuclear Fuels without fear of reprisal from you. He got that key, literally, shortly after I arrived the second time on the moon by creating a leak in Jones' offfice. It was Farnsworth who refused to give Jones his edysub bag until Jones handed over the documentation of Fellow's death."

"Interesting," said Barish in a calm subdued voice.

"It gets more interesting," said Mulvaina. "Both men underestimated your daughter's capacity for self preservation."

"She's really not much different than any other woman. Aren't all women into self preservation," interrupted Barish. Then he added, "The desire for self-preservation is an instinctive one. It's built into the psyche of humans. But I will say, women seem to have more of an instinct for it than us men."

Mulvaina thought Barish's interjection was slightly strange. Maybe a man's rambling to try to throw him off course. Mulvaina responded instinctively, "A human will resort to cannibalism to survive," he said.

"Oh yes, the history tales," said Barish. "I read that too, about the famous Donner Party settlers coming to California in the mid-1800's. They got trapped in the Sierra Nevada Mountains in all that snow and when they ran out of food and some started dying, the others ate their bodies in order to try to survive."

"Yes, Yes. Exactly my point," said Mulvaina. "And you see, Mr. Barish, both men underestimated your daughter's capacity for self preservation. And both men were quite unaware of the fact that your daughter had a badge which would make her invisible to the Astro-Four Security System. A badge I must say you gave to your daughter."

"Me," stated Barish.

"That's confirmed," Mulvaina simply said.

"Go on. Continue," said Barish.

"It was Rachel who killed her husband, Farnsworth, because he was going to betray her." Mulvaina paused for a few moments so Barish could absorb the full context of the words. Then Mulvaina continued, "It was Rachael who killed Jones who had been a continuous irritating source of liability for her." Mulvaina stared hard at Barish, but could not detect any emotion in his face so he continued, "Then Rachael's instinct for preservation went into full play and just to be on the safe side, Rachael also tried to kill me along with an entire shuttle full of innocent people. If it had not been for the skill of Joe Grimaldi, your daughter would have certainly succeeded."

Before Mulvaina could add more, Barish broke into the conversation. "Well, that is a very fascinating tall tale Mr. Mulvaina. Too bad it does not have a shred of evidence to support it. I do appreciate the information about Farnsworth and Southwest Nuclear Fuel. It will make its acquisition that much simpler. Please specify S.N.F. on your billing to Grogan. I will make him aware of why it will be noted in such a manner. For the rest of the bill, I expect to see some modest fees. Am I clear? I hired a detective not a fiction writer."

Mulvaina cleared his throat as if dirt had been thrown in his face. "I'm afraid, Mr. Barish, that your daughter's instinct for preservation was right about me. She had a right to fear what I was discovering or concluding about the building mishaps on the moon and the murders taking place on the shuttle runs back to Earth and on the moon base. Yes, even though she didn't have any real evidence that I knew the truth, her instinct to know that I could be her worst and most dangerous enemy was in full alert. For you see, unknown to me, Fred Jones had succeeded in giving me the original," Mulvaina reached into his shirt pocket and pulled out a key and held it forward, "of this key plus, of course, supporting evidence." Mulvaina reached into his pocket again and this time pulled out a sheet of paper neatly folded into quarters. "Here's a copy of Jones' statement I took from his safety deposit box," he said and after unfolding it, he placed it on Barish's desk. "Now, Mr. Barish, I am a private detective. I was hired by you. I can give you a choice."

"What kind of choice? Are there multiple endings depending on my choice? Or are you Mulvaina the devil I sell my soul to?" asked Barish seriously.

"The devil is a liar and the father of all lies. I am a private detective and a damn good one. My intelligence and courage comes from hard work and inner personal strength, thank you. I was hired by you and, therefore, I offer you a choice. You either release your claim to the lunar tritium and have your daughter discretely, but immediately and permanently committed for mental illness, or I take the original of Fred Jones' statement to George Carver, my friend at the F.B.I."

Barish stared blankly at Mulvaina and then down at the paper on the desk in front of him. "I can't read this small print. I need my glasses," he said as he began to open his top desk drawer.

Like a flash of lightening, Mulvaina's mind saw a gun. He leaped across the desk just as Barish was withdrawing the small black revolver. They struggled briefly behind the desk then the sound of gunshot blasted through the air. Barish stopped struggling. His face filled with pain. He dropped the gun, clutched his side, and slumped down back into his chair.

The door of the office swung quickly open. Barish's secretary stood frozen at the doorway. All of the color drained from her face.

"Quick. Call the paramedics," Mulvaina ordered. Then he added, "Barish has accidentally shot himself!"

CHAPTER 31

Mulvaina handed Thomas a beer. "Here it comes," he said and he stepped towards the t.v., picked up the remote and turned the volume up.

"Now, this breaking news," said the middle-aged anchor man. The camera zoomed a close-up of the Barish logo. "We are here live at the headquarters of Barish International where Ted Grogan, a spokesman for Barish International, the company which is the prime contractor for the Lunar Base Camp Project, also known as Lunar B.C., has just finished making an astonishing announcement. Mr. Grogan has revealed that Barish International has discovered vast deposits of tritium enriched ores on the lunar surface. These ores were discovered not far from the lunar base. Barish International has relinquished all claim to these ores stating these valuable ores belong to the people of the United States of America. Mr. Grogan stated it was the intent of Barish International to assist America's space agencies in a vigorous project to mine and ship these ores back to Earth for use in the struggling nuclear fusion power industry. Reliable sources close to the nuclear power industry predict that these newly discovered ore deposits will revolutionize the nuclear power industry here on Earth. It also predicts profit returns will pay back the massive investment in both space exploration and nuclear fusion research by many billions fold. Indeed this is an extraordinary discovery and an exciting announcement that heralds the beginnings of a new bright energy future for America and all of mankind."

The t.v. screen flickered for a quick few seconds and then the close-up image of the President of the United States of America shaking the hand of a young man filled the screen. The anchor man's voice continued behind the scene, "Now accepting congratulations from the President of the United States for Barish's monumental tritium discovery and humanitarian gift to America and mankind is Michael Barish. Michael Barish has recently taken over the management of the Barish empire while his father, John Barish, is recovering from a recent accident. No details on the accident at this time, but we understand that John Barish will be back to business soon. Well, that is the extraordinary news of the day. I repeat for those of you just tuning in now, a large amount of tritium on the moon has been discovered by Barish International and all claims to it have been given as a humanitarian gift to the people of the United States of America."

The anchor man's face faded and a young female Asian news reporter continued, "Now on the financial scene, stocks are surging after today's space find announcement. The Dow Jones industrial average has climbed at the moment to 619.09 points. The Standard & Poor's 500 index gained 72.4 points. The Nasdaq composite has gained 190 points. All energy stocks across the board are soaring. European and Asian stock markets are also all sky rocketing. It definitely is clear that traders are reacting to the historic breaking news."

Mulvaina reached for the remote and turned the t.v. off.

"Well," said Thomas Helms, "Thanks to Ted Grogan we received the check for our payment in full for all services rendered. It came by private courier just a few hours ago. I guess he wanted us to have it before Michael Barish shook hands with the President. This check will sure balance our budget for a while."

"That's good. Very good," said Mulvaina. He walked over to the window and looked outside. He did not see what he was looking for. He turned and walked over towards Helms. "What are you planning on doing tonight for fun, Thomas?" he asked.

"Actually, I have a big night planned. I told the wife to get a babysitter and I would take her out to dinner and uptown to a live performance."

"That sounds interesting," said Mulvaina. Then he asked, "What do you like about live performances?"

"At first, I was uncomfortable at live performances, but the wife loves them. Now I do, too. I find it a powerful medium for communicating shared human physical and emotional experiences. It makes art exist in real space," said Helms.

Mulvaina laughed. "Real space. Is that in comparison to outer space." Mulvaina laughed again. "Yes, I know there's been a cultural shift in the 21st century towards more interactive modes of communication."

Helms interrupted, "Like approaches engaging the viewer towards active participation in artistic production."

"But as a detective," continued Mulvania, "I feel I am sort of the engaged viewer in a life drama production all day and all night when I am working on a case. On my off time, well, my idea of a good time is being in a quiet place, so I can rest and refocus and reflect. An especially good time is sharing quite time at home with someone special." Mulvaina shifted his stance and then walked again over to the window and looked outside. After a few minutes he saw a yellow taxi pull up to the curb. The driver got out, walked to the back right door and opened it. "What a beautiful sight," Mulvaina said as he saw Julie step out of the taxi. "Go on home now and get your wife, Thomas, and take her to the best restaurant and live performance you can find tonight. It is on M.F.P. Associates."

"Hey, thanks a lot Robin," said Thomas Helms and without a minute's hesitation he was out the office door.

A few minutes later Mulvaina heard the expected knock on the door. He opened it and there Julie stood, sweeter than any angel could possibly be, he thought. He blurted out, "I know a little quiet café where we can get something to eat and then we can take an evening walk and look at the stars…."

Julie interrupted in a soft poetic voice,
"Silently, one by one, in the infinite meadows of heaven,
Blossomed the lovely stars, the forget-me-nots of the angels."

"Henry Wadsworth Longfellow," she said.

"From Evangeline" A Tale of Acadie. It's one of my favorite poems," said Mulvaina.

"Impressive," said Julie.

As they left the office the night sky was brilliant in its beauty with a supermoon. Mulvaina and Julie stood on the sidewalk looking up at the oversized moon that had come so close tonight to Earth. "After spending most of my life wandering the world looking for you, imagine I found you on the moon," said Mulvaina. He smiled and watched Julie's eyes as he spoke.

"I love you," Julie whispered and she put her arms around Robin's neck and hugged him gently. In the warmth of Julie's arms, Robin Mulvaina felt a flame of joy that made him speechless. No more words were needed…their hearts knew that beyond the Earth, beyond the moon, they would build their own world…together.

THE END